BY
PADGETT
POWELL

*Edisto*

*A Woman
Named Drown*

# A

# WOMAN

# NAMED

# DROWN

# A WOMAN NAMED DROWN

## PADGETT POWELL

*Farrar Straus Giroux*

NEW YORK

Library of Congress Cataloging-in-Publication Data
Powell, Padgett.
A woman named Drown.
I. Title.
PS3566.08328W6    1987        813'.54        87–248

The author is most happy
to acknowledge an award from
the Mrs. Giles Whiting Foundation.

*For Sidney*

*and*

*Amanda Dahl,*

*two tough girls*

# A

# WOMAN

# NAMED

# DROWN

❦ / Six months ago a friend of mine and I left doctoral programs in chemistry under certain different circumstances. Tom, a true scientist, got a letter at Oak Ridge, where he was finishing up his degree, informing him he had a job for the taking in Alabama—a high-level, nuclear police-chaperon affair, to judge from what he gleefully told me. I, scientist by default, by process of elimination, got a letter from my girlfriend in Norway letting me know in the subtlest, happiest way imaginable that I would not be joining her there as we had planned upon completion of my degree. When you are told that your fiancée, a promising post-doc to an internationally famous crystallographer expatriated from Brooklyn, finds that sagacious mentor "a cute little guy (only five three!)" who "eats eggs on his hamburgers!"

3 /

—you can read all the handwriting on the wall you ever need to read. I called her up, twice (once, as the rhyme puts it, for the money—$300; and once for the show—a considerable theater of her releasing, in a two-hour transatlantic tear burst, from the gunny sack of our entire six years off-and-on together, every crime of impassion I committed, and these transgressions I admit were endless, ranging from birthdays forgotten to old lovers not forgotten), and got a picture, as you can only on a telephone costing you a month's stipend, of her veritable sainthood for having put up for so long with the entire sham she convinced me I was, and was certain, as I reluctantly hung up the second time, that I had lost the finest, purest girl ever there would be for me. The starch in my doctorate will, which had not been much to begin with, vanished.

I trudged around the lab more bowlegged or splay-footed toward purpose than usual for about two weeks, when I got a card from Tom in Alabama. Tom is the sort of natural scientist who can learn, say, Schrödinger, while penciling Walt Disney characters in the margins and filling their balloons with the integrals and derivatives required on the following day's examination, and the first thing I saw on the card was a Goofyesque figure clearly representing Tom holding a Geiger counter to the rear end of an armadillo. Around the card this same figure pursued armadillos in odd attitudes and circumstances.

4 /

# A Woman
# Named Drown

With a magnifying glass—Tom can put, he claims, four thousand words on a postcard—I made out this:

*Remember Elaine? (Good girl.) I married her. Sold tent. Sold Mustang. It was a good car. Goofytom is doing what he does. Did you know armadillo feces register most accurately low-level hot traces around reactors? Me neither. P.U. Have my own desk. Partially stuffed mouse in drawer, lower left. Story behind that. Cotton sticking from his eyes makes him look like a ghoul mouse.*

> *A badge and some ID papers have been found belonging to a certain . . . no! yes! . . . Fenster Ludge. Colleagues plenty Silkwood-worried.*

The ghoul mouse refers obliquely to one of our maturer pastimes together before he moved to Oak Ridge (I stayed in Knoxville). We shot rats in our apartments with his slingshot. They (the apartments) were owned by the same notorious slumlord, and we found this competitive exercise preferable to registering formal complaints about the infestation. Neither of us wanted the rents to go up, either—Tom for true want and I for false (I was, still am, for that matter, abjuring some more or less family money, of which I am supposed to lay claim to plenty, but that is a longer story). The tent he mentions is one of two army field hospitals we bought for twenty dollars apiece and wadded cumbrously into our respective rat squats, providing thereby our rats with rich, paraffiny tunnels to hide in and our firing ranges with good, solid, gratifying backstops. It was almost as good to get a loud canvas *pop* as it was to get a rat.

Tom created Fenster Ludge when he discovered that one carrel in a suite of eight was empty. He made out a nameplate for the empty space, provided Fenster with some of his own books and supplies, and then began to ask his six new colleagues in the suite if anyone had seen "this Fenster Ludge guy." No one had. I caught Tom unable to contain a giggle one day during a discussion of the Fenster Ludge guy, why no one had seen him, etc. Someone finally claimed to have spotted a fellow fitting the presumed description of a man who might be called Fenster Ludge. And now he has taken Fenster to the sinister zones of nuclear cover-ups.

This card brought me somehow full circle to the Norway letter of two weeks before, and without feeling too bad about *that* per se (I don't think), I did feel bad, wasted. I sat for a bit and then did a significant thing without needing to analyze its merits, without needing to run the customary assay upon its advisability and consequences, short term and long, and self-actualization costs. I quit chemistry. I put Tom's card down on a heavy slate table and walked into Dr. Friedeman's office and said, I quit. Doctoral resignation is not standardly done—I have seen men thrown from offices, one nearly hurled from a balcony—but Friedeman took it like the godly sufferer that he is.

"Son," he said, standing up and taking me by the shoulder, "when the fire for inorgany that is in your heart reignites, come back. There'll be a place in the sun for you." I chuckled at this, and Friedeman did, too. We shook hands.

Friedeman was a card, and probably the one good scientist in the country with sufficient crazed grace to accept for long a dilettante like me. He was, on the side, a lay Baptist preacher, all disappointment to him a designed trial from God, so in a way I could hardly have presumed to have disappointed him. Try as I did, I could not imagine him delivering low religion, for his science is virtually high Anglican if not Catholic in its reach and style. He was capable of saying, "We know *full well in our hearts* that this bond is not less than three angstroms," and this faith could well be responsible for three years of failing, dogged experimentation to prove the improbable. For proving the improbable, and for thereby discovering the unknown, he is regarded a dean of inorganic chemistry the world over, yet he walks around his lab blessing beakers known to have contained winning results, pocketing lucky magnetic stir bars.

We shook hands, and I almost doubted myself, but kept going, kept quitting, quit. I walked out into the bright afternoon feeling truly released, as if out of the army or prison, and felt this relief most oddly for not having known before it any real oppression. I do not yet know the components of the feeling, a kind of deep-breath, first-of-spring freshness.

I met two women in the Smokies one night who told me they had been elementary-school teachers and quit, secretaries and quit, and presently they were stewardesses and thinking of quitting that. I remarked that they seemed to do a bit of quitting and one of them snapped, "You have to *start* before you can quit." I stood there on the bright catwalk wondering what I'd started, and why, and why I felt so very frisky.

What I'd started, as near as I can tell now, is a kind of *fit* of starts governed by nothing except a dis-taste for plans. For a casual, relaxed fellow with, as I have confessed, a bit of money in the closet, I suddenly came to realize I had a network of plans about me as stifling as the web of ambition any good young law student or medical student has, and I completely did not recognize the need for it. This money: no big deal; the old man would like for his drilling-supply business to remain in the family and that is me and that is about a two-million-dollar net thing and it had not particularly appealed to me *yet*. I had been occupied, I suppose, with a kind of disguised rich boy's finding him-self before assuming the obligation of the family for-tune, and I had been doing it as correctly, I thought, as

I could (that is, by not using any of the money, by doing nothing to endanger its source, by "applying" myself in some uphill and admirable endeavor the meanwhile, if science still can be said to be uphill and admirable). It must have occurred to me during the transatlantic jilt and upon discovering Tom's little predicament that I was doing not much really at all in the way of finding myself, which phrase I do not relish; and I was not doing much, anything, in the way of *having fun*. Rich boys ignoring their money ought to have fun.

So what I started that day was apparently a series of impulses which qualified for my interest if I could detect no point in them at all. I got a job sewing giant tents, learned to box, moved in with a woman who's a sometime amateur actress.

My training in science was not wasted: I can smell plans where there are none and so avoid them. In any good lab you look down about a two-year tunnel of programmed proving every rare day that you could possibly be said to begin anything, and even the chance that you will *not* prove what you hope to prove is planned for, accommodatable by an existing plan for happy accidents. And my training supplies me this: I sit every morning now recording these planless times, taking these notes with a near-Ph.D.'s mechanical care. I have a last blue-gridded notebook and I sit at a wire-mesh patio table and try to effect some shape, some contour, from these raw data of the wasty wonderful days since I quit. I quit the tent sewing and the boxing. I started the actress-living-with. I quit my room—gave away everything in it. I started these notes.

✵ / **B**efore I got to this major starting and quitting I did some warm-up starting and quitting. I started going to revivals and quit, I started to seduce the Orphan and quit, I talked for the very last time to the Veteran, during which time I decided to quit making fun of him. I did all this the night after quitting Friedeman, and some of it is not inexplicable. The data point of the spontaneous taking in of a tent revival, for example, has to do with getting home and breathing the waxy air of my field hospital and wondering about Friedeman's preaching, and seeing my cute deco dimestore-framed portrait of Miss Dr. Eminence in Love with Polanski looking sexier and smarter and righter than ever, and needing something to do other than make a third phone call. Before I could get going to the revival, the Veteran started yelling at his dead nigger.

He was stomping around hard in his steel-soled jungle boots, presumably trying to shake the dead nigger out of hiding. This was customary. As was not customary, I went over to have a look. I usually waited until he came to my room (next to his) to ask me if I'd seen the dead nigger.

Before I could knock, he jerked open his door.

"What!" he said.

"I'm here to help you catch him."

"You've been in my *house*?"

"No, man. No *way*, man. I've been *listening*." This was a somewhat standard exchange for us, a kind of password ritual.

"Catch who, then?" (This was also: my answer would help corroborate the existence of the prowling dead nigger.)

"The dead nigger."

"Dead nigger is *right*," he shouted, turning and marching into his room, gesturing wildly, his arms swinging with violence and surrender at once. "Every time I leave, dead fucking nigger pisses all over the place."

Under his open window was a puddle. It was water, rainwater, but it would not do to tell the Veteran this.

"The sonofabitch," I said, pulling a long face at the puddle. I overdid it—a hair too much sympathy tended to alienate him from its source. He became suspicious. There was nothing to do for it now.

"Does the *radio* bother you?" His clock radio was on, low.

"No."

"I'll turn it fucking *off*, then." He landed on his bed on his knees and violently twisted the radio off. I'd been in a few of these minuets with him before and had discovered it a mistake to change course. To tell him now that it had been noisy as hell and to thank him would deepen the suspicion and send him on a new, uncharted rant. Once he asked me how I liked his mother.

"The radio was fine," I said.

"If it bothers you, just speak up! *Say something!*"

"O.K."

"O.K., fucking-A."

We both pondered the puddle.

Standing there, having quit over at school, for the first time I was willing to try to understand this madman, to find out what had happened. Before, I had been willing only to play with him in the interest of an amateur knowledge of what I presumed was paranoia. It is funny how a little uncertainty, a little petty love-and-life dislocation like mine, can give you pause, tune you quickly to the genuine losses around you.

I knew enough not to ask anything remotely like what happened. All I could do was stand there and regard the puddle with him. He was calming down. I noticed I had not come with my hunting knife, which I always did—fully drawn and kept between the Veteran and myself to not the least distress on the part of the Veteran. I was talking to the Veteran unarmed.

I wondered how I'd look with something like a little true mileage on me. I noticed for the first time what the Veteran really looked like: he was handsome. You couldn't tell how many times his odometer might already have been around. He was not quite a bright, careful boy.

There was finally a bit of powerful logic in this dead-fucking-nigger thing, too. The rooms—all of them—did smell like piss, and the smell did seem to strengthen when you were away, and the Veteran's puddle was perpetual, whereas my window, always open, never seemed to take in rain. And the Veteran had absolutely nothing in his room to steal except his cheap clock radio, which is the perfect inspiration for a petty thief to foul things. Standing there with him, I thought finally that his truest touch was in believing his tormentor dead: I half thought there might be something to it all whenever he said *dead*.

The only sense this makes is to see the scene and its effect on me as what we call an energy of activation in the long series of planless, purposeless goings-on that followed. I have been occupied since all the quitting began with people who are anything but custodians of their chances in life.

I am determined to draw a curve through these

plotless days which will make order of them, to force a spline accurately down along the roller coaster of nonsense I started riding when I left the lab. A giant component of the reaction series I can hazard now (living with Mary, and having so splendid a time I wonder where I was but here all my life) has to do with women, with what my real relation to them is and is to be. For surely Miss Dr. Eminence in Love with Polanski was right. I was wrong for her, I was wrong to her, I was wrong with her. And I have a few suspicions that the wrongness is something not simply personal between me and her. I have some reservations about—I shall hazard a very early hypothesis, as only a false scientist would—young women in general, about this whole teasing setup. Which setup I needn't attempt to describe yet. What happened next falls precisely upon the curve of this function I would describe.

❦ / **I** quit the Veteran and his room. In the hall I ran into the Nurse, as I called her then. I call her the Orphan now, for what was about to go down. The Veteran was yelling something at the dead nigger. "Y'all find him?" she asked.

"No."

"He's tricky, I bet."

Ordinarily I would have complied with some eye rolling and offered to tell her some Veteran stories, but having gone and got righteous, having gone in there unarmed, half looking for the dead nigger myself, I failed to respond. This was timing: for months I had stumbled around in this hall trying to locate a natural opener with this woman, whose full head of red hair suggested to me electric sex. We had passed, nodded, paused, resumed, slipped into respective rat ranges across the hall from one another a hundred times. Now we were talking, and I was not going to talk. She rested a load of books on her hip and said, "You want a beer?"

"Yes."

I followed her in. She went out of sight and came back with two beers and her mail, which she tossed through at a table, kicking off her shoes and rubbing her stockinged feet together. I saw that she was in not a nurse's uniform but a simple white shift, the only thing I'd ever seen her in. I sat down and pretended to be comfortable.

"Just crap," she said of the mail.

I suddenly got the notion she had been crying a short time before, when she turned from me, crossed the room, turned back, and fell like big timber onto her bed, one arm behind her head and the white dress high, the red hair wide and fanned and brilliant. Her room was as drab as mine except for her hair. They were alike except for her hair and my tent. Thoughts like these kept me from feeling too conspicuous sitting there as she began a series of deep sighs.

"So," she finally sighed. "Tell me about yourself."

"Like what?"

"Like where were you born, who are your parents, that sort of thing."

"Who are my parents?"

"Yes. Of course." I should have left.

"Who are yours?" I asked.

"I don't know." She said this with such gravity,

such theatrical weight, that I refused to respond with suitable alarm.

"You're not a nurse," I said.

"I'm in history."

"You're in history."

"Yes."

"You're in history." She was getting impatient. "Hmmm," I said.

"The art of conversation isn't what it used to be."

She was somehow managing to raise the hem of the shift and her tits into relief without seeming to move. As badly as I wanted to leave, I couldn't, and as badly as I wanted not to be led in this programmed exchange, I was led.

"You don't know who your parents are and you're in history."

"Look, big boy—"

"O.K. I'm sorry."

It was better now that she had bucked up a bit and stopped the miserable sighing. I felt in a way she was as fragile as the Veteran, whom we could still hear stomping. I sat there, and unprompted further, she began a fluid account of her life history, without offering me another beer. She had been adopted and raised by a wonderful couple, whom she estranged by seeking as a teenager to discover her true parents. Along the way, virtually disowned by her hurt foster parents, she found herself in mean straits. She was an eighteen-year-old go-go girl in a strip club in Baltimore supporting a clod in medical school who left her, etc. I suffered something like an embolism of testosterone picturing her dancing naked in a cage with her head afire and breasts awhirl. She was sighing again. She was in history, she now solemnly announced, "to assemble the skills necessary to discover my true identity."

I tried bravely to cooperate. "Why is that so important to you?"

She looked at me with a certain, quiet horror. "I don't know who I *am*."

"You're you," I offered brightly, and got more of the look.

"No. What if my parents were—*coal miners* or something?"

"Oh. I see."

I didn't see, of course, but the Veteran, yet stomping around in his enraged search, put the notion in my head that she was in pursuit—and for all I knew, it was literally something like this bothering her—she was after, in a way, her own set of dead niggers. I sat there looking at her, the only body in the place not after a dead nigger. She was extremely good-looking, *extremely* good-looking.

"So. You. What about you?"

*She was extremely good-looking.* "What if we skip that?" I said. "What if you don't know anything about me except the *as is*?"

"Nooo," she said. "That's weird." She took another

gargantuan sigh. "There's been just *too much weirdness* in my life."

I wondered if it would be too much weirdness to cross the room and lie down on top of her, as every gesture of hers for the last twenty minutes suggested one should, and decided it would be.

"Thanks for the beer."

"You bet."

She did not get up as I let myself out. She lay there like Theda Bara, looking at the ceiling, pondering her lost parents.

♥ / **I** was charged up. I wanted to go to a revival across the river for reasons then and still not altogether clear, yet now I can detect some order in all the disorder. I am not certain that life itself is not some complex series reducible to its hundred thousand discrete reactions between reactant A and B yielding product C and D with this or that energy consumed or released to yield E and F from C and D, and so forth. I left the Veteran in pursuit of his dead nigger and visited the Orphan, a silent-screen actress in pursuit of hers, and in three weeks would be living with a true actress. In between, I went to a revival, ostensibly to get a look at the inside of a tent—Tom and I had never erected our monstrous units, each larger than the rooms they were wadded into—and what I saw was a conglomeration of folk all as desperate for phantoms as the Veteran and the Orphan, and all arguably after a dead man who might never exist for them. There were not a few actresses present as well, the real kind that central casting never gets. They were rolling on the ground, for the most part, being held gently at their crotches and breasts by a man with a copperhead.

After my day, I was not in a state to be further amazed, but I was further amazed. A smallish man—I took him to be about the size of Polanski—in a blue double-knit suit was screaming at near the pain threshold into a whizzing, hissing, scratchy public address system. How many years will you be in hell? he asked the congregation. The congregation was uncertain. He offered to tell them. "Pitcher to yourself a 1," he yelled, "and foller it with *all the zeroes in the world,* and that's how many years you'll be in hell."

The congregation held its breath. All the while the preacher was drawing zeroes in the air with one hand and holding in his other, calmly aloft, the copperhead. I neglected to follow the sermon, but it soon had its effect. Suddenly the man was on his heels discreetly feeling women rolling on the ground, touching the snake to them. One woman got up, brushed herself off, returned to her seat, located her purse, lit up a cigarette, sat back in her chair, and told her companion, "Go on, honey, get called. Nothing like it in the world."

"I don't know," the second woman said. "Them things—"

"*He'll* hold that thing, honey. It ain't nothing but Satan's *failed little messenger boy.*"

I looked at the docile copperhead, sanest fellow in the room, proving by not biting anyone how the truly damned are saved. I was starting to get high—high, I suppose, on the number of improbables that seemed to be appearing before me. I liked the feeling. Dreaming through more polyester loudness, I pictured to myself a 1, with all the zeroes in the world representing an endless chain of unconnected, connected events—my new theory of the human life reaction series. It seemed that I had been wasting my time by not acknowledging this necessary connectedness of the unnecessary things one can do in a life. I could do all the things in the world I wanted to do, ungoverned by imposed criteria for serious living, and they would connect, evolve, according to unalterable laws that were operating as surely as the one that popped Newton on the head with the apple, that made Mr. Millikan's oil drops swerve, that made Herr Kekule's snakes bite their tails and roll overnight into the benzene ring.

All I had to do was get loose in the limbec of life. A voice from this local, queer providence came to me from a row behind: "Did you know Camel Tent hiring, Jimmy?" I turned to look. Jimmy said he didn't know and didn't want to know, because Penny Baker sewed four of his fingers together and his (Jimmy's) wife now had a good enough job for the both of them. "So why fix it if it works, right?" Jimmy said, and his friend nodded Amen.

I stopped at a snack joint on the way back over the river and watched the movie of just too much weirdness continue to play before me. A guy stood at a picnic table punching one of those fist-held cutters into a box top of onions. He was crying from the onions. From inside the joint came a voice: "Just because your dog died, it's no reason to cry." Some laughter.

The guy threw his cutter into the onions and wheeled on me. "I caint take it!" he said.

He came nearer. "I can do the *job* they want, but I caint take a joke!"

It was possible to believe, looking at the tears streaming down, that they were not all onion-induced. He was breathing hard, truly worked up.

"You just got to grow up," the kitchen voice came. "Dogs die." Howling in the kitchen.

The onion chopper ran to the serving window and raised it and yelled inside, "I *caint take it!*" He tore off his apron and threw it in the dirt. He looked furiously at me. "I just caint take a *joke*," he said again, somewhat calmer.

"I don't blame you," I said. "I can't either."

"You don't understand." He was the Veteran stateside.

"You're right, I don't."

That satisfied him.

I slipped home, got in without spooking anyone.

# A Woman
## Named Drown

I had nothing in my life not to take, but liked the attitude. I'm not taking it either, I thought, when it comes, and maybe it has come and I have been taking it—maybe dilettante chemistry and bright girlfriends in Europe and inheritances hovering overhead are taking a lot of it. Tom's hunting armadillo shit. Crackerjack nuke-whiz Tom, Fenster Ludge in tow, is taking it, and I'm not.

I wanted the Orphan badly, but not enough to take it.

☙ / **T**he next morning I set out into old Knoxville for Camel Tent and passed on the way the woman I had passed for years who watered her garden every morning. She looked at me, surprised, I imagine, to see me walking in the opposite direction from that she expected of me. She waved. I waved back. I could not have known we had begun a correspondence. I did notice her, however, a bit more closely than ever before. She was got up in a brilliant turquoise robe and wore sufficient bright makeup to herself resemble a giant flower, and around her were a thousand smaller blooms of carmine azalea and purple iris and katydid-green leaves. Upon this dazzling garden she held a spray of nickel-colored water in a long arc from a fat red hose. I could see that she managed the spray by using her index finger over the hose mouth—I had an aunt who did that, the only other person I've ever seen do it that way. It was a bit of a riveting detail, and perhaps I looked at her too long. She waved again, and I waved back again.

I could not know, as I said, that we had begun a program of overland communications, and I didn't know I was waving to Knoxville's star actress, and I quite didn't expect to be moving in and setting up a base for recording these my lab notes of life. I was hell-bent on getting down to Camel Tent and securing some form of income to replace my paltry but regular stipend.

Once there, I argued for an hour about my surfeit of overqualifications to sew tents until I had a job sewing tents. When I sat down and hit the foot pedal and saw a hundred inches of cord shoot through cotton duck as heavy as a duffel bag out of a needle as big as an ice pick, I had no trouble recalling Penny Baker sewing his four fingers together. Near me a man was announcing how we were to distinguish male from female rattle-snakes. "You all better listen to this," he said, concentrating on his stitching. "It's valuable."

"Shut up, Sweetlips," a second man said from a nearby machine.

"O.K., fine," Sweetlips said. "*Don't* find out. I could care less. But the fact of the matter is females don't have any poison and if you know *that*, you're safe." He bent to his stitching.

"Tell it to the new girl."

# A Woman
## Named Drown

"Do you know how to tell a female rattler?" Sweet-lips said to me.

"No. How?"

"They don't have any rattlers." With that he placed a large paper cup on the floor under his machine and pissed in it from his sitting position. "They don't *pay* me to lollygag half the day in the head," he said. "So I *don't*." He reminded me of the Veteran—I'll turn it *off*, then.

I sat amazed at the synchronicity of these things— pissing on floors, nuts, snakes everywhere, tents—and amazed at how *correct* they seemed, fitted together in a matter of hours with an overwhelming sense of orchestration that seemed to satisfy whatever urge bade me walk out of the laboratory. I felt fine, a fine idiot doing a fine idiot job, listening to fine idiot patter.

"The new girl's O.K.," Sweetlips said, after a while, to the other man. "I been watching him. Don't fuck with him or I'll kill you."

The other guy said, "Right, Killer."

When the shift ended, Sweetlips and the other guy took me to a place called Bilbo's Bar, Gym & Grill. In-side, we sat at a lunch counter on stools facing a box-ing ring. We ordered beer. Sweetlips said, "We come here to watch the niggers beat the ever-living shit out of each other." He winked. He winked with an exag-geration reminiscent of a cartoon wink, signifying what irony I could not guess, because I took him at his word.

Presently the other guy, whom Sweetlips called Roach, said to me, "So tell us about the new girl."

"The new girl doesn't know her ass from a hole in the ground," I said.

"That's exactly what I said the minute I saw you," Sweetlips said. "Didn't I, Roach?"

"No, you were talking about rattlesnake pussy."

"You think that's a lie? Anybody'll tell you that. The female has no rattlers. New girl, isn't that a fact?"

I looked at Roach. He was indifferent to all of this.

Sweetlips leaned over me to Roach. "The new girl's all right. I repeat: Don't fuck with him or I'll kill you."

Two blacks started sparring. Roach said, "Shut up. This does me good."

We watched the boxers work. One of the guys was as solid as a live oak, and after a couple of rounds he came over to our side of the ring and said to Roach, provoked by nothing I saw, "Fuck you, too."

"You going to take that?" Sweetlips said. "I wouldn't."

"Kill him, then."

"*I* would."

By my reckoning it would have taken an army of Sweetlipses and Roaches to even pin the dude.

"I'm as strong as that nigger," Sweetlips said.

"Jump him, then."

"It wouldn't be fair."

# A Woman
## Named Drown

I came to understand, during my brief tenure at Camel, that Sweetlips did two things, at all times tried to do two things: he proffered preposterous lies, making everyone present appear to believe them, and he boasted of his strength, which was perhaps a subset enterprise of the lying. One morning he announced that a pygmy rattlesnake had the dimensions of a short link of country sausage, showing us how long and how big around with his thumb and forefinger. On another occasion he claimed to have spotted a pygmy deer. "A *full-ant* ten-point buck no higher than a beagle!" No one challenged him on either pygmy, and he went on sewing, visibly more content.

On the issue of his strength he was even more hyperbolic. One morning he came in greasy, telling us he had on the way to work stopped and pulled a woman's Ford engine out of her car. "It saved her a garage charge."

Roach responded to this one. "Bledsoe," he said, "there's a string hanging out of your sleeve."

Sweetlips looked at his T-shirt sleeves, finding no string.

"Oh," Roach said. "I'm sorry. It's your *arm*."

Sweetlips jumped up, knocking over a tumbler of piss. *"What! You don't think I'm strong!"* He ran to Roach's machine and grabbed it and tilted the entire affair—Roach with it, the chair is connected—up about a foot off the ground, until Roach said, "O.K." It was not an idle feat—the machine must have weighed three, four hundred pounds. Sweetlips's back, under his tight T-shirt, clenched up into a set of knots that looked like a bag of rocks and sticks.

I could have kept going at Camel. All I had to do was listen to Sweetlips and Roach do their camp and worry about Penny Baker fingers. I set up an interesting routine. I went back to Bilbo's and found a dude who wouldn't kill me and learned a little boxing in the mornings. The watering woman and I, you might say, fell in love waving. I flirted at a hundred paces, got beat up for three rounds, listened to pygmy hysteria for eight hours. It was not a bad time. My previous life, of soft-metal bonding mechanics, seemed no less preposterous than Sweetlips's life of pygmy sightings and giant strength. I was completely comfortable being completely out of control.

❦ / **I** was in fact beginning to feel like I was drunk but free of motor impairment. Whatever presented itself to me as partaking of the continuum of nuttiness was the thing for me. I would not act my age or observe my station.

Back at Bilbo's Bar, Gym & Grill the next morning I had coffee. The same massive dude was sparring, this time with a slighter opponent, who was having a bad time of it. The lighter guy looked ready to quit, ready to cry, for that matter, but did neither. At every break the oak tree called him a punk.

I looked around. The counterman appeared to have scoliosis. He bent to hear a customer and jerked back up, staring wild-eyed at the customer. "No!" he shouted. "No more bacon!" The customer smiled and went back to reading his menu. The counterman retreated in a huff through double doors, out of sight.

The boxers had quit. I did not see the smaller guy, but the oak tree was putting Royal Crown dressing on his head and then a lady's stocking over that. He picked up a load of gear equivalent in bulk to a rodeo cowboy's tack and left.

The counterman returned and I got a refill. "Who is that guy just left?" I asked him.

"StebbinsStebbinsStebbins what—you fall off the truck? You want me to tell you history all day or you want to be somewhere else? No b.l.t.'s, in case that's your next move."

That was Harold, the counterman. What he had told me—in two weeks I managed to decode—was that everybody who was anybody knew Frank Stebbins, who had a middleweight match in France coming up, and who was going to be history when it was over, and that he (Harold) did not cook bacon anymore. Ever.

The slighter boxer reappeared at the counter near me, began looking suspiciously all around the place, and said quietly to Harold, "A Curs."

More happily than I'd seen him all morning, Harold virtually ran a Coors over to him. "Shifty'll chew your black ass when he sees this."

"He ain't gone see shit. Stebbins most kill me." He took the Coors and poured it into a Coke can that he'd held under the counter.

"I'm looking for someone to spar with," I said.

# A Woman
# Named Drown

The boxer looked at me. "You botts," he said. "I seen you before."

"You've seen me drink beer in here, maybe."

"I recall it. Wid honks."

"Yes," I said, nodding solemnly, as if to deepen the confession.

He looked to the ring as if we had not been speaking.

After a while I said, "I guess you have to go with Stebbins, anyway."

"What you mean?"

"Nothing. Just that you spar with—"

"Okayden."

"Okay what?"

"Tamarr."

"When?"

"Sikserty."

"You can call me Al."

"Egret."

We tried to shake and got fouled up accommodating each other's racial handshake, and wound up fumbling our fingers together awhile. We were involved in this little charade when a small, gray-haired squat of a man came up and grabbed Egret's Coke can and threw it at Harold.

Neither Egret nor Harold said anything. The man stood his ground, rasping breath, the gray hair coming out of his ears and nostrils, his mouth stained olive by chewing tobacco. He looked at Egret.

"You conspiring to sign wid *him* now, or what?" He meant me.

"Haw, naw, Shif," Egret said. "He a bottser himself."

Shif—Shifty of Shifty's Stable, as I came to know—regarded me with a long squint. The hair was coming out of him in tufts, in whorls—he looked like a tobacco-stained owl. He took a deep breath. "You wear glasses!" he said.

I heard Egret do a little thing like a hiss under his breath.

"How long you wear glasses?"

I touched my glasses to make sure I still wore them and said I didn't know.

"You box, you see." Egret did the *siss* thing again. "Bottsin cure the blind. Tell him, Shif. S*iss*."

"Boxing cure the blind," Shifty said. "Look." He broke his eyes hard to one side, then back, revealing red-veined, oystery eyeballs. He looked up, down, whirled his eyes all around the sockets, following the motion with his protruding green tongue. It occurred to me I had seen this demonstration—on the sidewalk the day before, as Sweetlips and Roach and I came in. He had presumably grabbed a passerby, attempting to lure him in for eyesight correction.

"Boxing exercise the eyes, see? You ought to box for Shif. You sign wid anybody yet?"

He grabbed a napkin from a chrome box, pushing it to me with a ballpoint pen.

"What's this?"

"Sign this, you with me. We get a true contract when the time is right."

"Let me wait on this one, Shif."

"Don't wait until it's *too late*."

He turned to Egret and pushed the napkin to him. "You. Sign again. And this time, no more goddamn beer." Egret printed on the napkin with painstaking concentration WILLIE EBERT.

Shifty folded the napkin into his pocket and limped off.

"What's your name?" I asked.

"Like I told. Egret."

My time boxing was without event. Ebert was not good enough to teach or to hurt me, though I'll wager he was considerably tougher in the long haul. He was finally mostly a clown, very gentle in the center, and he was living in a tough, tough world. When Stebbins saw us pawing each other he yelled, "Punk and white punk. Punkpunk." It didn't bother me, but Ebert explained something to me later.

"When Frank call you punk, it's *race*. When he call me punk, it's *sex*."

I sat there, apparently failing to respond as he would have liked.

He suddenly offered, "Got two kids."

"What?"

"Two kids."

"Who?"

"Me."

"You?" I figured him about eighteen.

"Selfsame individual you see."

All I had to go on was the *race* and *sex* thing.

"They black?"

"Who?"

"Your kids."

"Dit."

"*All* black?"

"Dit."

"All right. Nobody's white, except me, nobody's queer."

"Dit."

"Except Stebbins."

"*Siss*. I hope the Frog eat his *ass*."

"You want a beer?"

Ebert looked around. "*This* early?" It *was* about 7:30.

"You better have one. Tomorrow I bust your ass."

"Oh. He serous. Okayden. A Curs."

When I left Bilbo's that morning I did not go to Camel Tent. I walked back to do some waving with the actress. We'd reached a peak of waving. We were, I figured, waved out.

❦ / **W**e had been waving now for nearly three weeks, and it was not the simple acknowledging of passersby. From the start, from that first morning I surprised her by going the wrong way, it seemed she had waved with a forthright openness that suggested we were not, to her mind, altogether strangers. It is unsettling to be acknowledged by a stranger who appears to think himself familiar, of course, and in this case, as I've said, the stranger was hailing me boldly in a turquoise robe, holding a forty-foot spray of water on a half acre of violently blooming color.

I recall once being waved at by a man in drag from a balcony window in Baton Rouge, and as I ignored him and kept walking, he shouted loudly down, "Well, it's only *hey!*" and shamed me. I gave him a weak, noncommittal wave that made him laugh.

The watering woman and I had fully explored the dynamic of stranger-to-stranger waving, and it had developed its own periodicity. I could have drawn up the elemental chart of waving. On a Monday she'd give me a haggard little gesture from very near her hip, where her free hand rested as she watered with the other, and I'd return in kind a little thing with a finger or thumb from near my pants pocket. By Wednesday she'd be offering more arm, more motion, with loose-wristed familiarity and a smile. By Friday we were at a quantum ledge of hand semaphore: she waved like a relative down at the docks to greet the ocean liner I was on. It made me respond by waving so vigorously in return I'd go off the sidewalk.

On this Friday she saw me coming, crimped off the fat red hose, and began to gesture so wildly I was certain she intended a slapstick parody of us, that she was saying finally, Well, it's only *hey*. She got her arm up stiff, not unlike a German salute, and swung it gravely over her head, leaning a bit with the motion as if she were signaling with a great, heavy, brass railroad lantern overhead. It was so far out on the chart I could not wave back properly. I walked up to her fence.

She gave the hose a further dip and crimp, and some water flew onto her robe, which she stared at, dabbing the spots into broader spots.

"That material will dry quickly," I said.

She looked at me. "I know how quickly this material will dry. I spazzed out."

I was aware that we had already abandoned the innocence of strangers waving at one another. It seemed a bit of a shame.

"I hope you're not standing there like a geek because you think I'm that woman named Drown."

"Ma'am?" I said.

"Ma'am *what*?"

"I think you might be what?"

"You think I might be a fool. Come on in and let's have us a gin something." She turned and walked into the flowers, from where, out of sight, she called, "Gate's unlocked." She called then, from inside the house, "Fizzes or will simple tonics do?"

I managed the gate and said with fake aplomb, "Tonic's divine."

"Divine is *right*," she called from the kitchen, where I could see her through a bank of jalousie windows which enclosed a patio. It had flowered oilcloth furniture and a concrete floor. On a table beside a yellow weatherproof sofa with blue hydrangeas printed on it I saw a Sunday newspaper entertainment section, the cover of which was a color photograph of a woman standing on a spiral staircase. Her hair blew to one side, and gray moss on oak trees blew in from the other. The colors of the woman's face were printed out of register, yet it was still recognizably the woman in the kitchen fixing gin somethings. The caption read *Mary Constance Baker in "A Woman Named Drown."*

"Some of these people get the idea you are what you act in the amateur theater game," Mary Constance Baker said, coming out with two drinks. "I have to wear a disguise to go shopping."

"Because you are famous here?"

"Because there are folk out there who think *I* drowned a plantation—mules, Ashleys, slaves, my mulatto children, and all."

"That happens in the play?"

"That happens in the play."

"Sorry I missed it."

"Sugar, play like that will be back every other year. Sit down."

"This is you," I said to her, pointing at her photo in the Sunday paper.

"Bingo." She was already through with her drink, shaking the ice.

"I hadn't seen this before."

"It's no federal case. You shoot pool?"

"No."

"Come on."

We went into a sunken room, which was walled on the garden side by glass blocks. The colors of the flowers came through softened and mixed so that the room felt as out-of-register as the newspaper photo. She racked the balls and started running them off the table.

"Where'd you learn to shoot like this?" I finally
said.

Not looking up from her shot she said, "My old
man."

"Where is he?"

She kept shooting.

"What happened to him?"

"What?" She interrupted a shot.

"Your old man. What happened?"

"Oh," she said, realigning. "Lost his stick." She ran
the table. She put her cue down and turned on a two-
tone hi-fi in the corner. "Ray Conniff," she said. "You
look ready." She left for the kitchen with my glass.

I could see her dancing to Ray Conniff and His
Singers as she made the drinks. She came back, racked
again, and started dancing from shot to shot, swooning
dreamily, then snapping up with eyes all business, sink-
ing balls with precise cracking collisions of incidence
and reflection, rolling in rocket trails of the candied
light.

I asked, without planning to, if I could take a
shower.

"No ceremony here," she said, indicating another
part of the house with her cue.

"Before I do," I added, again more or less surprising myself, "should you know me any better?"

"Like what?" she asked, looking up.

"I don't know. Job, name, sexual preference. That
sort of thing."

"I thought you kids did away with that song and dance."

"We tried."

"Take a shower."

In the shower, beautiful pink-and-green tiles seemed to move a bit along with Ray Conniff, too. I held my head in a big towel for a while and saw a double bed and without ceremony got in it, under a spread that had a thousand fuzzy balls on its fringe and millions smaller on its surface.

When I woke up—it was one of those sleeps in which you drool—I was out of the covers and people were talking.

"Well, you'd think a bitch named Drown'd dress before goddamn t'ree o'clock, for Christ sake," boomed a male voice. I heard Mary say, very formally, "What can I get you, Virginia?"

The door opened and Mary came in, motioning for me to stay put. "Guess what?"

"What?"

"A drop-in."

She slid out of her robe and into real clothes with her back to me. "There's two drawers of the old man's things when you want to come out."

She left and I got up. Not once do I recall wondering what in hell I was doing there, though now, looking back, it seems a good time to have wondered. Perhaps I was held by the certainty that I had to stay in order to find out. I tested my head with a small shake and saw my face was waffled from the knitted bed-spread. I looked like a kid up from a nap.

In one of the indicated drawers, I found the old man had left two kinds of pants: swimming trunks with built-in net liners and bright putter pants with elastic waists. The shirts were all pastel Ban-Lons. I did not see the clothes I came in. I found some white shoes. I emerged in a canary golfer's ensemble.

When I stepped into the den I was converged upon by the loud man, who introduced himself simply as Hoop and pointed out his wife, Virginia, as if she were down the block. Virginia waved vaguely to us while talking with Mary, who came over with a tray of drinks. Hoop and I took one.

Hoop had balls in play on the table. "Hey, bud, you play this friggin sport?"

"I don't shoot for shit." My language seemed to delight him.

"It's a bitch all right," he said. "It's a motherin bitch." He then missed his remaining shots, feigning dissatisfaction with himself. I thought he was going to ask for a game, but he racked his cue and came over to me, stopping within a whispery, conspiratorial distance. "Hey, Constance," he yelled, winking at me, "what's two sailors got to do get some liquor in these drinks, for Christ sake?" He quickly whispered, "You got a good one there—lotta the boys give a nut be where you are. You know what I mean?"

"Sure I know what you mean."

Hoop shot out his hand for a confirmational men's shake, and I shook it solidly. Still holding on to me, and pulling me closer, Hoop bellowed, "This boy's all right, Constance!"

Holding and squeezing and tugging me to and fro, he said again, "He's all right, he's all right." Mary came in bearing more drinks and a very patient hostess face.

"You takin 'm to Florida or something?" Hoop said to her. "He looks just like Sam."

"No plans, Hoop."

"What's your handicap, son?"

"I peg the meter," I said.

"Ha! Whorin Mary! I'm off the friggin scale myself. We'll shoot *thirty-six* sometime. That's how to beat you youngsters. Thirty-six. *Sudden death.*" He offered the handshake again. "Sudden friggin death."

"Let's go up with the girls, Hoop. I want to meet your wife."

"Blame you for that, I don't," he said. Tapping his front teeth with a fingernail, he said, "Perfect teeth." We went up from the sunken den into the bright patio.

"God*damn* if you aren't a green thumb to beat the friggin band, Connie," he yelled as we entered the undiffused, flowery light. He opened a bank of the jalousie windows and beheld the garden, stooping a bit to look through the slits. "Jesus the rumrunner, would you look at that?" We both looked through the slits.

"Remind me to cut you a spray, Ginny," Mary said

to Virginia, who stood by smiling. She did have perfect teeth.

"Oh, please—" Virginia said.

"No, it's no trouble. You know me: Too many glads in the glasshouse."

"Goddamn. Trouble, my purple baboon *ass*. She's *got* to cut 'em down, honey. Need someplace to *walk* in this friggin Amazon."

"It's my pleasure, Ginny, it really is."

"Thank you, Constance," Virginia said.

"Hey! Friggin idea! You gals go out there and mow some friggin parrot jungle down and the kid 'n me makes a round."

Hoop rushed toward the bar, a substantial rattan-and-hardwood thing I hadn't noticed, dusty in a corner of the patio. Virginia and Constance went out with a pair of shears.

"Would you look at the dust!" Hoop yelled. "Find me some swabbin gear, Chief."

I went in the kitchen, made us two drinks, and returned with a rag and soap. "She's been making them in there."

"I know, for Christ sake. Broad's got this bar from the islands, beautiful friggin teak here, won't *use* it. We take it apart and hide it on board and get it here and *get it back together—that's* the friggin miracle, and *tight* when we busted her up—no friggin numbers on it like your dinosaurs and shit."

"Where was this?"

"Mutton fart capital of the world."

"You were in the navy?"

"Guam, Guadalcanal, one of them G islands. No, Seabees. All them islands is alike. This bastard could've come from the halls of friggin Montezuma. What the shit difference. It's heavy, pure-quill teak, we stole it from an *operating whorehouse*, we *got* it here is the thing. Contrabandits! Joke!"

Hoop threw the rag and soap bottle at the bar's small chrome sink. "Whore called Five-ton sits on it, crying, see? Because Stump and me are having at it with screwdrivers, see?" He goes into falsetto. " 'I love you, Joes, no shit, Joes, but need post office for sell love.' Five-ton whines this at us, see? Imagine that: some wiseheimy tells 'em a friggin whorehouse is a *post office* and they *buy* it. 'You want first class, Joe?' It was a scream. 'You want special delivery?' There Five-ton is, trying to hold the bar down, crying, and Stump and me start pulling it apart. Beautiful." He is wiping the bar with great, broad strokes. I already feel drunk again. Hoop's rag is steaming in vigorous circles on the teak.

"Doesn't come over here that he don't wash the *friggin* bar," Mary is suddenly whispering in my ear. I have the sensation that some time has passed that I missed. Hoop is furiously twisting a dish towel inside a glass.

"It's his *past*," Mary says. She rolls her eyes. Virginia comes in with flowers, looking for a vase, her perfect teeth apologetically out front.

Hoop squeaks the rag in his glass and holds it to the light. *"That's* a clean glass," he says. "Something about a *really clean glass*, eh, Chief?"

Virginia passes through the room again, still looking for a vase.

I had the feeling that time was lurching and braking and bouncing me around within it. Ray Conniff and His Singers, for one thing, were suddenly very much with us, and I seemed to be swaying along with Mary to them.

"Always use your twist on these," Hoop said, grinding a lemon rind around a glass rim. "People never follow their friggin *recipes.*"

I jumped because of breath in my ear. "How's your clutch?" Mary said, inches from me.

" 'Ere you go, Chief." Hoop plunked three new drinks squarely on fresh cocktail napkins in front of us. "From the bar, where they ought to be," he said proudly. Mary blew smoke at him and took a stool next to mine. She put a finger into the waistband of my putter pants.

"Hoop," she said, "you're a goose." She was tugging at the waistband in rhythm to Ray Conniff and His Singers. Hoop squinted at her. She shook ice at him.

"Excuse me," I said.

On my way to the bathroom I saw Virginia's spray of shrimp-colored gladiolas on a marble stand and was drawn to them like a huge, clumsy bee. My face went in—lipstick corals and green leaves as delicate as nylon. Virginia was, I then saw, taking a nap on a daybed a few feet away. She looked patient, flat on her back, serene, her teeth concealed.

When I got back to the bar, Hoop and Mary were squared off about something I got the feeling was well rehearsed.

"If it *had* sunk it would still be all right," Mary was saying.

"Sunk?" Hoop boomed. "Aboard the *U.S.S.*—"

"Too much that *should* sink *never does!*" Mary intoned, slapping the bar with a flat-palmed crack that made Hoop jump. She put her arm around my shoulder.

Hoop winked at me.

I said, "Hi, Poop. Hoop."

He tried to take my glass.

"Have you gathered," Mary said, again inches from my ear, "that my old man and Hoop won the Second World War holding hands?"

"Sort of."

"And I imagine a young man like you has been around, too."

"I've not been a man named Drown." Looking back, I see this remark could have been tasteless—I still don't know that her husband didn't drown—but it was innocently said.

"Funny," Mary said.

"Do you do that stuff for a living?"

"Ha," Mary said, motioning for Hoop to light her cigarette. "That's community theater I do to get out of the house."

Hoop lit her up and she blew a big spiral at the ceiling, watching it as if she had forgotten us for a bit. "My point is, the world doesn't go around on biographies. Remember that and we'll get on fine. No bio."

"I will." I had to recall the Orphan.

"Act!" Hoop suddenly shouted. "That's about *right*. Chief knows more than he looks. She *acts*, all right."

Mary looked at Hoop. "Ensign Hooper here believes in quartering on board while in port." She held her cigarette near her ear, smoke swirling irregularly up around her hair.

She looked at me with low eyelids. "What do you intend to *do* about Mother Nature?" she said.

Hoop stopped his fussing with bar things.

"I'm not sure yet," I said.

"Mush!" Hoop said. "We're out of ice." He went to the kitchen.

Mary leaned toward me, as if falling, and pressed her forehead to mine, holding me behind the neck with her cold drink hand. She rolled our foreheads together.

"How do these work?" Hoop stood in the door with a blue plastic tray of ice cubes. "There's no arm."

"Twist them, Hoop," Mary said.

"There's no arm," Hoop said again.

"They don't make arms on them anymore," I offered.

Hoop looked at me. "Yeah, I see."

I took it for a slur. "You torque them, Hoop," I said, trying to somehow slur him back.

"Yes, Hoop," Mary said. *"Torque you* ice trays." She made the sense I couldn't. She was holding some liquor. She laughed.

Hoop turned and retreated. We heard ice cubes popping loose and hitting the floor.

"Friggin torque is right." Hoop came back and fitted the new cubes into the glass-lined ice bucket. As soon as he settled them in and achieved a tight fit with the lid, Mary held her glass in the air to him, tapping out her cigarette. I started to swivel away from the bar, but she got me by the waistband and tugged me back around.

Hoop hurled the ingredients of another drink toward a fresh glass. He scrubbed the rim with lemon rind. "Always your friggin twist on these," he said again. Mary looked at the ceiling. Ray Conniff was skipping.

"Goddamn, Connie," Hoop said suddenly, leaning toward her over the bar. "You don't respect—"

Mary pushed her stool away and saddlebagged herself over the bar, reaching a set of keys which she retrieved in a violent, upward fling. She marched into the kitchen. Hoop said, "She's going to tear a page now, kid."

We heard a roar from the kitchen. In the garage, through a door off the kitchen, we found Mary in a high, boxy, old Mercury, revving its engine with a thoughtful, deliberate expression on her face. We stood next to the car with our drinks, smelling the exhaust. Mary floored carbon out, deafening us. She got out and gallantly held open the door, to me.

"Jesus," Hoop said.

"Don't say a damned word, Hoop." To me: "Get in."

I sat where placed, fingering the large knurled steering wheel of the Mercury. Mary crossed to the rider's side. Hoop attempted our old conspiratorial leer behind her, but it fell and he suddenly yelled, "*Go* to Florida!"

"Fine," Mary said.

"Friggin Jesus."

Our eyes were stinging.

"I got to get Virginia *out* of here," Hoop proclaimed. He trailed a V sign into the house. We heard him yell, "Evacuate!"

Beneath the moldy smell of the Mercury was the smell of a showroom-new car. I eased it out of the garage into heavy rain, which knocked dust off the hood in violent spore bursts, leaving craters of fresh, new color. It looked for a moment as if we were driving on the moon.

The car was so high-centered and heavy it felt full of water, full of water and horsepower. I got it up to a speed which brought in some wind, and looked over at Mary—her hair flying about like the photograph in the newspaper she swore wasn't her. *I* was on a tear, full of gin and with a woman named Drown, and I drove us to a club called the Car Wash, where I knew Ebert to hang out. A naked woman hand-painted on the outside of the club spoke from a cartoon balloon, NO DRINKIN ON PREMISE PLEASE. The artist had given her very large breasts, using, apparently, a house brush that lent them a hairy aspect.

Ebert came forward with a gaping kind of frozen grin on his face: *This is so absurd I can't quite laugh and I can't quite ignore it*. And we *were* in an all-black club. "Man!" he said, when nearly to us.

"Man what?" I said.

"I ain't never *seen* you like this before."

"Like what?"

"On the *week*end."

Mary rolled her eyes. She retook my arm, and Ebert turned back toward the bar as if to shepherd us through the quieted crowd. The noise slowly resumed, and we went to the bar.

Ebert was not sober. "Man," he kept saying, "you a *trip*."

Mary whipped a little flask of gin out and asked the barman if it was all right.

"*She* a trip, too," Ebert said. His eyes were brilliant and looking over my head, as if he was checking the horizon. Mary had the barman pouring her a drink from her flask, which he put away for her. They had no tonic, so she took a 7-Up and the first hit made her wince. She winked at Ebert. "My main man, Ebert," I said to her, indicating him with a thumb. The jive felt very artificial and I decided to cut it out. Ebert and I were better friends when we couldn't manage to shake hands.

"You a trip," Ebert said again. "Never *seen* you like this."

He was still studying things afar, eyes wet.

Watching him, I lost some time. I suddenly noticed Mary at the pool tables. She selected a cue and stood, hip out, chalking it.

"Ebert," I said, "do you have loose teeth?"

"Naw, man," he said.

He didn't want to know why I would ask him something like that. I could not have told him. Something about his dreaming, teary gaze suggested old men without teeth, and I thought I saw him clenching his jaw as if moving his teeth.

"Your teeth are tight?"

"They tight. They loose, too."

Mary had gotten into a game.

I motioned with three fingers and pointed to Ebert, myself, and Mary, and the barman gave a quick nod upward and filled the order. He carried Mary's fresh gin and 7-Up to her and she gave me a theatrical scowl.

Ebert put his head down onto the rim of his glass, and when he raised it he had a dark ring imprinted on his forehead. "Never *seen* you like this."

He was drunker than I cared to see him as our escort. I gave Mary a little let's-get-going sign.

She had made friends by amazing all the dudes

anywhere near the table. A guy came up to me. "You carry her *back* sometime."

We drove home. The Mercury felt like two or three boulders.

In bed I had the spins. I started deep breathing to burn up some alcohol before throwing some up, and got a saliva run.

"Put your foot on the floor," Mary said.

"It's on the floor," I said. "I know about that."

"You know a lot," she said. I couldn't tell if she was mocking.

"What do you call the bedspins?" I asked.

"The whirlies." I had thought maybe she had an exotic name from her own generation. She reached over and felt my forehead then, as if to say she had not meant to sound sarcastic if she had. I lay there spinning, thinking: She maybe thinks I know things, and maybe knows I don't.

꿿 / **S**o that is how I find myself sitting at this wire-mesh table in the mornings, taking hangover notes, reflex motions of a would-have-been scientist. Since that first day three weeks ago we've not had anything so spectacular as the drop-in. Hoop and Virginia's visit established several data points:

1. Sam, or Stump, is presumably dead, and that is the extent of my privileged knowledge.

2. He may have had something to do with Florida, where it is, as if in obeisance to Hoop's outbursts, somehow tacitly assumed we may go, so long as it—the going—does not obtain an urgency. There is a sense in which we are packing our things psychologically, and when the moment is right, but not demanding or in any way special, we will take off and simply be there

as unprepared and innocent as we were that night in the Car Wash.

3. The no-bio rule is a constant of this universe. You follow it if you want to operate. What I know of Stump and Mary is largely known, and she is indifferent, as she says, to any bio song and dance out of me.

Mary is moving through rich banks of azalea, her head alone above the creamy reds, nickel arc of cold water lobbing heavily all around her. I have begun reading her old acting scripts. They turn up everywhere—in Stump's clothes, under table legs—and they all seem to have been handled roughly. I have not found one yet with its cover intact.

I don't know plays beyond the forced college stuff, and I've never seen anything like these things. In every one there is a role made for Mary. I found this in a script under Virginia's daybed—cover gone, as usual—and was stupid enough to ask Mary the title. "I forgot," she said.

JASMINE: Mother, John took me up to Black River and we went swimming.

MRS. TAYLOR: Are we getting a bit too familiar, Jasmine Ranelle?

JASMINE: Oh, Mother! It was nice. You know, the water is so dark, and when we jumped in, the splashes were white and foamy, like—like the head on an A&W!

MRS. TAYLOR: Like the *head on an A&W!*

JASMINE: Yes!

MRS. TAYLOR: Jesus my beads.

Mr. Taylor had been shot in a hunting accident and Mrs. Taylor could not be too careful of her daughter and only child. They went round and round over gentlemen callers, with Mrs. Taylor becoming gradually more mannish and violent in her protection of Jasmine Ranelle. Mrs. Taylor could even swing an ax handle!

Mary, I imagine, played a grand Mrs. Taylor. Late in the second act she cracks a suitor over the head while he's kissing Jasmine—with the flat side of a butcher knife. The audience sees her creep up on them through a scrim, the knife is shadowed hugely behind them, and Mrs. Taylor shrieks into the parlor and *slaps* the caller with the knife. Suitor flees stage.

JASMINE: You ruin *everything*, Mother.

MRS. TAYLOR: I used the *back side* of it, honey.

JASMINE: That's what you *always* say.

I had notions of Mary surprising me with versions of her characters—say, the knife trick sometime, but she never did, of course, and was generally not in favor of my associating her with her roles, as our introduction on the lawn had suggested. She was not in favor of anyone mistaking her for a play character.

I had a role to consider myself. Guy, young guy, stops by, moves in, shoots pool, and drinks gin wearing widow's husband's pastel golf outfits.

MRS. TAYLOR: You don't know a *thing* about a *one* of those *young men.*
JASMINE: That's the *point,* Mother. I'm *getting* to know them.
MRS. TAYLOR: You're *getting* nowhere!
JASMINE: And you're seeing *to* it!
[*Runs, crying, to her room*]

Mary has trundled by with a wheelbarrow blocked from sight by a bank of azalea. When she slides into view, I see the straining tendons in her neck. Sweat is on her like rain. She is not far from the gin flash point.

She'll come in, and all the gentle care of plants outside will translate into a ruthless hammering of ice in the kitchen. She uses a chrome gizmo which serves, screwed into respective configurations, as a jigger, a corkscrew, and a hammer. On her way to shower, she will deliver a drink and a hard kiss, holding my neck with the back of her cold hand, leaving me to contemplate the scene. The drink sits tall, emerald lime refracting through sparkling soda, on a queer blond split-level end table with splayed conical legs and rusting brass feet.

Yesterday I suffered the momentary illusion that I

was progressing at pool, but I am finally only mastering a more manly look of indifference to the trouncing. You would think her cruel in this if you did not see how absorbed she is, oblivious to even Ray Conniff and Perry Como when she gets a challenging run. She would be mean, I think, only if she *were* capable of pulling back in my behalf.

After pool Mary asked if I was any good with figures and I said fair and she handed me a desk-style book of checks, which she explained was "a bit behind." It hadn't been balanced in eighteen months, there were checks missing, there was a statement showing automatic deposits from two sources which I was told were regular. I made the bold presumption that they were Stump's pensions of some sort and determined monthly cash flow, within a tolerance of three hundred dollars, and figured the account to be breaking even or gaining slightly.

Mary came out in a waxy wig that frightened me.

"Want anything from the grocery?" she asked.

"What is that?"

"My disguise."

"For what?"

"Theatergoers."

"Come on."

"You've read the play. Give me a check."

"Give me a list, I'll go. You look like a wick."

She shrugged and I went shopping. I had indeed read the play. If she was telling the truth about people recognizing her and mistaking her for the character she played, I could believe that they would harass her. They could hardly not.

The woman named Drown was charged with manslaughter (forty-three counts) because she had failed to relocate her shanty town away from the river. A large flood swept her plantation into the Mississippi and to the Gulf.

DROWN: Negligence! Was I negligent standing on the second floor of my house in a nightgown fighting water moccasins? Was I negligent when I saw my cash box float out the window?

PROSECUTOR: You were negligent when you did not inform your colored workers of the imminent danger.

DROWN: What was there to tell? They could see it was raining. They knew damned well how high the water was—they were at the river day and night salvaging bateaus and wagons and whatever else came down. They were getting *rich* in trees over the water with gang hooks, hooting and laughing. You don't know a damned thing about poor niggers if you think they would have listened to a rich white woman telling them to abandon a rolling mint like that river.

[*Jury whispers among itself; judge calls for order*]

PROSECUTOR: No further questions at this time.

This speech turned the tide in Drown's favor. She was let off on the manslaughter business, which, it seems, had been only a thin pretext for exposing the real issue: she had two mulatto children drowned in the flood, who were allegedly hers by a black worker named Carlisle. What implicated her was having taken two *other* children—fully black ones—into her home the night of the flood. This survival of only two of the four children on her place gave credence to the town talk which for years had rumored her to have had twins, no less, by Carlisle, a big handsome man who sometimes worked as her chauffeur.

PROSECUTOR: Were you not in St. Louis for a period of five months seven years ago—seven years before two seven-year-old children were *allowed* to drown on your property while two others were saved?
DEFENSE: Objection.
COURT: Sustained.
PROSECUTOR: And was not your place run at that time by—
DEFENSE: This line of questioning is irrelevant.
COURT: Can the prosecution prove this questioning related to the specific charges?
PROSECUTOR: We can.

And so Carlisle, otherwise uneducated and ill equipped, had run the Drown place for five months. (The name Drown is the character's real name, and the playwright seems to have been either ignorant of or delighted by this heavy-handedness.) Apparently his overseerage was competent, for a large crop of high-quality tobacco was harvested, and Carlisle, in his pride, was seen in town smoking self-rolled cigars so large he was dubbed Havana Carlisle. Retrospectively, it was argued that the cigar-parading was evidence that he knew of his mistress's birthing business in St. Louis.

Drown beat the rap, but Mary Constance Baker had more trouble with it. She was convinced that a part of the audience—the mall ladies who recognized her, for instance—believed she slept with blacks. Thus I have come to do the banking and the marketing, as she calls it.

I got back from shopping and it occurred to me for no reason that we had taken another invisible step toward our undeclared trip to Florida, where I swear we are somehow bound to go, whether vexed by Hoop to do so or not. I've had my drunk-driving skills checked, can count money, and now have demonstrated some kind of real-world dexterity in fetching three bags of groceries five blocks—these are the talents of secular dependability required of a companion on the road, it would seem, at least in my imagined itinerary of our imagined traveling together.

We had a steak on the garden patio last night and we got on the oilcloth-covered chaise together, Mary sitting in my arms, and upon a casual remark of mine about the flowers, she said, "It's too cold for them in winter here." In my no-bio disadvantage, a remark like that indeed suggests Florida, and I think I suggest

Stump, whose clothes fit me to a *t*, and I think, all together, we're in small maneuvers for leaving for Florida,
but there'll be no song and dance about that either.

"Thought I'd go see an old friend tomorrow, if
you'd like to go," Mary said.

The idea of being alone in her house seemed radical. "Sure."

"They're a gas. Hazel and Bruce."

"Okay."

She turned around, and up and kissed me so suddenly she reminded me of a girl nervous about sex and
deciding to get the butterflies over with. I felt young,
too: Stump's Ban-Lons give me a strange feeling on the
skin, not unlike I'm wearing ladies' nylon hose. The
garden was close and green and dark, and a sprinkler
was *spicking* somewhere, casting a mist on us. Mary's
skin has a half-size-too-large feel, giving it a satin effect,
a softer touch than a younger woman. It is hard to
imagine we want to leave at all. It is a halcyon, un-
judged time: billiards crack, drinks fizzle, colors pour
into the house from dazzling flowers every morning
watered, making it a cozy, gauzy life, as if we were
candied fruits sweetening in a snifter of brandy.

☙ / **H**oop and Virginia were practice, it turns out, for Hazel and Bruce. Mary put a half gallon of gin in the car and handed me the keys. On the drive, out into an old suburb development, she said, "Sugar, these people are somewhat rough-cut."

"What's rough?"

"Hazel is a doll, for my money, but you might be startled." I resolved not to be.

We found a low, cinder-block, brown house with rotted turquoise eaves and a rusted-out screen porch. A woman I presumed Hazel swung open the screenless door to the porch and bent over a bit, squinting through black cat-eye glasses before rushing Mary, chortling and pumping elbows. Their embrace was a confused arrangement and an ongoing adjustment of Hazel's cigarette and Old Milwaukee and slipping eyeglasses, and Mary's gin and cut flowers and Honeyhow-longhasitbeens and Honeyhowgoodyoulooks. When introduced, Hazel looked at me and then said to Mary, "I see what you mean. You lucky dog. If I was twenty years younger . . ."

In the house she sat us in the kitchen at a redwood table with benches. She put a tray of ice cubes and two jelly glasses on the table and sat down opposite us, still in a can't-believe-how-good-you-look-long-it's-been stream of talk, and Mary poured our drinks.

A flushing noise introduced Bruce from the bathroom, and he came in, fiddling with his fly. When he saw us, he bent sharply over and zipped, then walked over to his place at the table, which was marked by another Old Milwaukee in a circle of water and an ashtray.

Hazel stood up and kissed him, having to hold her glasses in place, and Bruce also had to restore his glasses high up onto his nose with his middle finger. He held them there while he bent down to a Styrofoam cooler on the floor and got two beers, then looked up at us and got two more, and Mary said, "We brought our own, thanks."

"I'd give my eyeteeth," Hazel said, "if I could still drink hard stuff."

"Doctor told her it 'ud kill her," Bruce said. Hazel kissed him again.

The girls went into old times, which were privately hilarious, while Bruce and I watched each other drink.

# A Woman
## Named Drown

After about twenty minutes, old times had become current events, and they had nothing currently in common except the visit, so Bruce and I were acknowledged. Hazel turned to him with yet another smacky kiss misaligning their eyeglasses. These kisses seemed designed and sufficient to make up for centuries of neglect. She held her lips to his cheek while he held his glasses in place.

"Do you know what this rascal did on our first date?" Hazel suddenly said. "He takes me to this bar outside town and says we're going on to another one ten miles away, so I better go to the can."

"Seven miles," Bruce said.

"Yeah. So I go in, and there's this nude poster of Burt Reynolds *naked*, right where you *have* to look when you sit down. And there's a *board* over his pud."

"His what? I never heard you call it *that*." Bruce sipped his Old Milwaukee, settling it back on the table in a circling motion.

"You're about only a foot from it, right in front of you," Hazel said, "and the killer is, it's big—the board is *much* bigger than it needs to be. *I'm not moving that board*, I say, and for a long time I don't, and then I forgot and damned if I don't. When I do, I can hear this roar go up in the bar."

Bruce adjusts his glasses, smiling.

"The sonsofbitches have a red light wired up to the board which goes on when you lift it," Hazel said. *"Our first date."*

"She comes out and they have it so the red light is still on, and everybody says together, How big is it? It was funny."

"And do you know what else was so funny, Mary?" We were laughing. "What?" Mary asked.

"They time you."

"She had a good time. Forty seconds. The record's five minutes on a girl that was sick first before she could look."

"Our first date! What a stunt. Come over here, honey," Hazel said to Mary, patting the table. "I don't ever get to see you." When she got Mary seated, she took her hand and held it in both of hers and patted and held on to it on the table. Bruce got up and came to my side of the table. Mary was watching me.

"Now listen to what I done to *him* on our *second* date," Hazel said.

"This *was* pretty good," Bruce put in. I had the feeling they were their own full-time archivists, historians of Old Milwaukee moments, as much as they were anything else on earth. They were amazing. One side of Bruce's face was a giant lipstick smudge from Hazel's endless kisses—they were completely happy, completely happy about nothing.

Hazel had picked up early on a thing Bruce said during the Burt Reynolds date, and she put it to good advantage on their second date. Bruce, when asked how it was going, was in the habit of saying, "I'm looking pretty good this year, don't you think?" Hazel had him take them to visit a friend of hers, and during the normal early conversation the friend asked Bruce how he was.

"He don't say, I'm fine, like he ought to," Hazel says. "He's still cock of the walk from the damn red-light trick. He pipes right up, Well, Hazel here thinks I'm looking pretty good this year, how about you? And my friend says, I can't tell, Bruce, I'm blind. It like to killed him. She *is* blind."

Hazel is laughing and Bruce is nodding with a kind of red-handed smile on. "He's so full of himself he doesn't even look at her! She's waving her head around like Ray Charles and he don't see it! Hav-A-Tampa Bruce!"

"She calls me that because I'm from Tampa. She thinks it's funny." Bruce smiled what I was coming to consider his polite smile.

"You ought to be flattered," Hazel says. "Them things are *big*." She roars.

"You made a mistake that day, too," Bruce now adds.

"I sure did," Hazel confesses, beginning to giggle, and again I think they are interested in the record more than in the events. They want to get these stories out right. Mary is giving me a bit of the old Mother Nature look, as from the Hoop show, and I realize these are not unlike afternoons.

"A pretty good mistake," Bruce confirms. Hazel nods.

"A doozy," she says.

"What did you do?" I asked.

"We went in this convenience store on the edge of town after the blind date—we call it Bruce's blind date—and a girl I knew was working there. Well, I remembered her as being beautiful, and I saw her, and she smiled, and her *teeth* were gone. I said, *God*, honey, what happened to your *teeth*?"

Here Bruce collapsed laughing, finally losing his glasses.

"God, honey, I said, what happened to your teeth? She said, Nothing. I looked again and her teeth were *there*, but they were so *dark* you could barely see them. They were little stubs, all gunky and black."

"Like a bunch of sardines, or something," Bruce managed to get out, and whether it was truly funny or if I'd succumbed to the power of the archive, it struck me as the funniest remark I'd ever heard.

When we left, Hazel and Bruce remained seated at the picnic table and waved at us as we walked ourselves out of the house. The last thing I saw was Bruce pushing his glasses and Hazel kissing him on the cheek with her smacky lips full of overfresh lipstick.

On the way home I got the notion that we'd just gone to a play together, that this was sort of the kind of entertainment Mary had in mind if we went to Florida, and that I'd had a little audition myself with Mary watching me all afternoon. I now had apparently proved myself a worthy audience for the road show we would take in.

Mary and I sat out again in the oilcloth chaise, kissing like teenagers, her throat a soft, firm, pipey thing that amazed me more than anything had that day. I suppose I mean to say that Mary amazed me, but it was things smaller than the whole proposition that kept riveting me—her throat, her skin, her flowers, her smooth idle days, her nut friends, her no-bio. Her liquory, solid taste and lack of babble. It was the first time I'd ever been involved with someone without a large measure of something like dependence obtaining—"emotional dependence," the university psychiatrist called it when I consulted him about my growing European phone debt—and I say this of course realizing that I was by election almost dependent upon her in two weeks for even the food I ate. We were not maneuvering one another, we were striking no contracts, tacit or implicit. We were, to my mind, free to like each other and that was that. As I say, I found this amazing and still do. We could smell the entire garden, cool and breezeless.

"Florida has palms with T-shirt monkeys with rattle eyes climbing them, bombing Yankee white trash with coconuts," Mary suddenly offered.

"They have Yankee white trash?"

"Sure. Wear Bermuda shorts and long socks and hard shoes."

I took this to mean we were indeed going, and pretty soon. Leaving with her in her stagecoach Mercury seemed as radical as staying in her house by myself, but I supposed the going was just one more moment in the reaction series of life I had decided to subscribe to, so I told myself I'd best prepare to arrive in Florida dressed as the husband of a widow I knew not too well. If it was not pure coincidence that I read of Havana Carlisle one day and met Hav-A-Tampa Bruce the next, then elemental forces decidedly beyond my control were at work.

※ / I was not far wrong. Mary's pace in the garden changed, and she began transplanting some small camellias from a nursery bed to a permanent terrace. In general she started moving about like a nesting bird putting this here and that there. I decided to do something about my room.

I must have gotten a look of cogitation on about giving up my own place, because Mary suddenly called from twenty yards away, "What's the matter with you?"

"Nothing. Sorting things out."

"Please don't," she said, and went on with the camellias.

I went straight to Bilbo's and had coffee and found Ebert. He gave me a look of mock amazement. "Am I seen you *today* or *tamarr*? I thought you *retire.*"

"Been busy."

"I know. Shack up."

"Right. Get cleaned up and come with me."

"Not the Car Wash."

"No."

We went to my old room. I found James, the janitor, who called himself the factotum, and who was arguably the only normal human being in the place. When he initially showed me the room, he conducted himself not unlike a porter at the best hotel in the world, opening the door for me, crossing the room and opening the window, standing back to let me approve of everything. "You got a good view," he said.

The view was of an adjacent building's roof with a compressor on it. With a deafening screech, the compressor engaged. He did not flinch: he took a deep, satisfying breath, as if showing me the quality of good mountain air. "That radiator works," he said, "but the furnace does not," and laughed. "I am James, the factotum." Here he paused, as if to let me comprehend things, and I believe I did: for $85 a month, a man with a title like factotum would not be asked to fix anything like a furnace.

"Guy moved out down the hall," he then said, a bit conspiratorily, as though confident that I'd gotten his meaning so far and we could now begin to be intimate. "Come on."

I followed him to another room, in which he

showed me a cardboard box. In it were some books on Freud and a snorkel and mask. "You can have this shit," he said. "She will not know a thing about it." I would learn that "she" was the manager, whose desires and requests James took some pleasure in contravening. My accepting the books and swim mask was, I believe, my acceptance of his terms of operation, his not fixing things and grand title.

So I got James up to the room and introduced him to Ebert.

"Nice suit," James said, indicating my powder-blue togs.

"*Cold,*" Ebert said. "You a cold brother." James ignored him—I think he consciously repudiated all black blackness.

"James," I said, "all this shit is yours, and give Ebert what of it he'd like."

"What?"

"I'm through with this stuff."

"You are *what?*"

"There's that snorkel the other dude left. I'm leaving everything in here with it."

This felt wonderful, though at bottom it made me nervous: it was a room packed full of the dear trash we all get attached to, and you usually require a fire or a flood to rid yourself of it.

Ebert said, "Man, what you mean?"

James said, "Yes. I believe he is disturbed." He had

a penchant for well-enunciated, and sometimes abstract, speech. "It is a complex thing," he added. "I am amazed and amused."

Ebert picked up my basketball and palmed it aloft. "Man can't give all his shit away."

"You want that basketball? It's new."

"I see it *new*," Ebert said, using the emphasis to reinforce his assessment that I had cracked. He looked at the photograph of Dr. Eminence in Love with Polanski taped over my desk.

"This your *chick*," he said. He thumped it.

"You can have that, too."

"I don't even *know* her."

"I don't either."

James laughed at this and walked to the window from which he had shown me the view. Something in his attitude there suggested he had accepted the estate: the trip to the window was a sidelong inventory of the trouble and value of the inheritance.

Ebert dribbled the basketball, thundering the old, hardwood floors.

"Cut that out," James said. "Pick what you want."

"Take this off your hand," Ebert said, holding the ball. "And this." He got an electric alarm clock. "You a trip."

James and I were by this point in a fine, high, ineffable conspiracy. I was feeling physically lighter, and he was calculating profit, the overwhelming return on the worthless books and snorkel he had initially invested with me. He had categorized the stuff into boxed trash and pawnable goods.

"Fellows, it's been real," I said. James gave me a limp, earnest handshake. "Good lucks," he said. It was perhaps the only anomaly of speech I ever heard out of him, and I would not presume to call it an error, for it could have been his own correctly grammatical way of saying there are several kinds of luck.

"You too, James."

Ebert wouldn't look at us. From across the room, I offered him a power fist and left, taking only the large brass padlock I had locked the room with. I poked back in and told James to give my tent to the Veteran and waved again and was off. Crossing the Tennessee I dropped the lock into the water, where I could picture it landing softly in the mud, sending short brassy reflections into the murk, being nosed by carp.

Mary was still gardening like a demon. I made myself a drink and watched her.

When she still did not quit, I had the impulse to help. I ran out and volunteered to take the shovel. After some time of it, it seemed the gin, for once, was going to be necessary, and I saw again my lock interfering with the whiskery nosing of carp on the river bottom, and I was giddy about not having anything of my own in the world. I wiped my forehead, placed the shovel for another shot into the soil, and fainted. When I came to, I felt perfectly wonderful, entirely and unequivocally euphoric, and did not want to move.

Mary was standing over me. "You cut those camellias in half."

"Yes," I said.

"Can you get inside?"

"Yes ma'am."

"Make us some."

I made two tonics, and, correctly repositioned at the wire table, watched Mary finish up the garden, and after she did, we did not play pool. She started putting things in the Mercury, wearing a tall, angular towel on her head, looking like Queen Nefertiti.

My little faint seemed to have precipitated Florida up to the edge of happening, as if an "illness" was the final necessary requisite for a "vacation." I went to bed early and had visions of Mary's monkeys looking at me with plastic, rattle eyes, and orange and turquoise in nonspecific roadside glary scenes.

Late, or early—earlier, I now think, than I did when she got me up—Mary said, "Feel okay?"

"Fine."

"In thirty minutes, what's say, let's go."

She left the room.

I jumped up and dressed and got that cool, irritating feel of clothes on fevered skin. I found a sack and put Stump's suits in it and the playscripts. Mary hustled a last box of gin and mixers to the car, and we were off in a high-centered set of swerves, the Mercury rumbling like a tug.

Sometime in the certified wee hour, in fog, I saw WOODBINE GEORGIA on a road sign, and it got cold. Again, rising up, I saw GEORGIA GIRL DRIVE-IN, a green-framed trapezoid of wet plate glass, and in a blast CAMDEN ICE COMPANY, an old wooden loading dock with ice crushers on it. We stopped after crossing the syrupy St. Marys River and sat at a picnic table with a winged concrete roof, part of an abandoned Florida Welcome Station. Across the road were two abandoned motels and a liquor store. "I left the freeway, and we've been making time," Mary said. We must have left Knoxville just at dark.

I saw no palms, no monkeys, no fruit, no glare. A red neon WHISKEY shone from the liquor store.

As if reading my thoughts exactly, Mary said, in an affected redneck accent, "Me and Stump believed in a *differnt kind* of Florida."

We passed a strip of ruined nontowns, Yulee, Oceanway, Lackawanna. Old motels, those still standing, were either apartments or flea markets. Some were just rubble in a sandy semicircle of ragged palms.

❦ / In Jacksonville, Mary hooked a hard right, west, explaining it wouldn't do to go south too fast in Florida. I took to riding in the back seat, where things were agreeably peripheral, while Mary blared head-on into the panhandle. I could pin down all the things whipping around in the car and relax. Making a drink was much easier if you didn't have to lean backward over the seat, surprised by Mary's swerves and brakings. And I was free to sleep. I dreamed once of Bilbo's. Everyone was gloved, not only the boxers, but Shifty and Harold and a face or two I'd never seen—gloved, trunked, shod in tight, shin-high boxing shoes.

When I woke, the wind was stinging me with my hair, Styrofoam cups were flying about, Mary was eyes on the road. I picked up a playscript. It was the titleless adventure of Mrs. Taylor and daughter, Jasmine Ranelle. I read near the end.

Jasmine and the apparent ultimate suitor have barricaded themselves in the Taylor garage, a wooden building set apart from the main house. They are trying to start an outboard engine which is suspended in an oil drum.

JASMINE: It's supposed to have water in it, but this will be louder.

[*Suitor pulls starter cord*]

SUITOR: This thing's ancient. I'll bet it hasn't run since—

JASMINE: Since he died. That's just it. This was his motor. It was on the boat he was shot in. It kept running. It was running when they found him. In circles. When we start it, it will drive her nuts.

SUITOR: *If* we start it.

JASMINE: It'll start. They don't make them like this anymore.

[*Suitor delivers more pulls; a sputter, smoke coming from the drum*]

JASMINE: There she goes! [*Tiptoes to closed garage door and peeks through crack in direction of house*] This is going to be *wild*.

[*Two more pulls and another sputter*]

SUITOR: What if she doesn't come?

JASMINE: If she doesn't come, and buddyroe she's *going* to come, we'll lay down here and breathe fumes until we *die*.

[*Engine takes, producing deafening, reverberating roar*]

# A Woman
# Named Drown

I quit there: Mary virtually whiskey-turned us into an old stone gas station, sliding us through a parking lot of crushed white shell and pop tops to a dusty, billowing halt not too far from a man sitting in a metal lawn chair.

"I hope you got a license to drive like that," he said. "Not many do."

"Bathroom," Mary said, getting out.

"Ladies' is out," the man said. "You look like you can handle thuther."

He winked at me. Mary headed for the men's room and I opened my door, spilling cups and plastic ice bags and hamburger wrappers.

The old man said, "Fillerup, son?"

"Yes, sir," I said.

He winked again, starting to move.

He pumped the gas and sat back down; we waited for Mary. I went around finally to check on her. The door was open, commode in view. I walked on behind the station. There, under a giant oak, were men in chairs. I had stopped just clear of the building. All of them looked at me, stopped talking. I was in my canary suit. I walked on to let them know that I might be dressed unusually but I was not shy. Most of them were old, the kind of downright geezers who go to great pains to cultivate looking old—leave their teeth at home, don't shave, walk with canes that don't appear necessary. And some of them were a generation younger, old tush-hogs between hell-raising and geezering. One of the tush-hogs said: "You drink beer?"

I sat at his table and flicked a piece of Styrofoam off my yellow pants. "Yes," I said.

"All right," the tush-hog said, and the talking under the tree resumed, several men already engaged with Mary.

"Go on with it," my tush-hog said.

A geezer said, "Where was I?"

"You was at the court-martial."

"Right."

"This is McCrae, bud," Tush-hog said to me, indicating the geezer. "He's telling the story 'Parker McCrae and the Screech Owls.'"

"I could shoot a squinch owl in the dark backward with a *mirror* if I'da had to," said McCrae.

"We know. Get on with it."

"Where was I?"

"They didn't believe you could identify the thief, because it was dark."

"It was *dark as hell* and can't nobody say it wasn't."

"Nobody did. They said it was dark. That's why they said you couldn't identify the thief."

"It *was* dark."

Tush-hog looked down at his beer and then up at no one. He looked at the geezer. "O.K., it was *dark as shit* out there, Parker."

McCrae nodded sharply, once. He leaned forward on his cane. "So I had to *prove* 'em I could see good

enough out there to name *names*. So I said, Come
on tonight to a spot I know and bring me a good .22
rifle."

"And they did."

"They did. And we got there, and I knew there was
at least twenty-five squinch owls in them trees there. I
asked them if they saw any birds in them trees. No,
they didn't. I told them to clear the ground under the
trees and to look for the birds up close when they was
under."

"And they did."

"They did so, yessir."

"So you then picked off twenty-five invisible
screech owls."

"Not so fast. Twenty-three."

Here, Tush-hog looked at me with a little sign of
mischief.

"I shot five times and I told them to go get them
five birds. They lay 'em out there."

"At the feet of the brass."

"Lay 'em out and counted 'em and I shot five more
—*kicke kicke kicke kicke kicke*! Like that."

"That's ten."

"They was all just standing there and I wasn't sure
they believed me yet. There was . . . Where was I?"

"Ten birds down, fifteen to go."

"Not so fast. Thirteen. I can see better in the dark
than most in the day." Tush-hog put his face in his
hands.

We waited. Mary's table was laughing at something hilarious of their own making.

"So I shot thirteen more and let them other two stay. They couldn't see 'em anyway, so why not? *Conservation*," he said gravely, "that's the thing now."

"You won the case," Tush-hog said.

"Boy *confessed* when he seen me shoot them squinch owls. Started blubbering about like a *dia*per gal."

Tush-hog looked me over. During the story I had noticed an old Coke box on galvanized pipe legs with iced beer in it, and I got up and got us three beers. "How do you pay for these?"

"You don't," Tush-hog said. "It's a club."

McCrae snapped his beer open and went for it by leaning forward to meet it on the table.

"Bobby Cherry," Tush-hog said, swinging his hand over our beers, and he tried to crush my hand, but wearing canary Ban-Lon got me ready for him, and he did not crush me. I toasted McCrae and the screech owls.

Mary got up, sailed over to us; Bobby Cherry stood up, I didn't. "Handsome," she said, "you ready to go?"

"Yes, ma'am," I said. I stood up and tucked in my shirt. If there's anything dorkier than a man wearing a yellow golf suit behind a filling station with a bunch of the boys in their jeans and pearl-button shirts, I suppose it's a man wearing a yellow golf suit with the

# A Woman
# Named Drown

Ban-Lon shirt tucked in and the pants drawn up high showing a lot of sock. This was Mary's method: she effected a little drama under the oak by charming the men and then leaving with the fruit she called handsome, and it was my job to look even more geeky to further tweak them. She had done something of the opposite with me in front of Hoop.

The car was still where Mary had slung it. She paid the man in the metal chair, fired up, and we were off in a cloud of rocks and pop tops. I picked up the playscript.

[MRS. TAYLOR *flings open garage doors.* JASMINE *crosses her arms, juts her jaw at* MRS. TAYLOR. SUITOR *holds his nose and his ears, and moves about garage as if looking for clean air to gasp*]

I was finding it hard to hold in mind the hypothesis of these days, if hypothesis is not too ludicrously grand a term for my reaction-series theory of life. It occurred to me that untenability is contained in the nature of the investigation: these days, these characters, have at their center no center, no towardness. I'm not putting this well. I mean: Mary is never Mary.

And the fools I've been meeting are not *consciously* themselves. And they are happy. This is just beginning to come together for me, and I'll leave it in this rawest form. Data: Mary finds insupportable the awful singular role of Stump's widow; she becomes Drown, Mrs. Taylor, boozist, lover, teaser of roadside redneck. Friedeman found insupportable the awful earnest singular path to scientific truth; he saves the damned from hell, on the side, with Baptist hysterics. These are the brainy ones. Those less burdened are capable of distracting themselves from artificial singularity without trying: Sweetlips, chronicler of pygmy, believes less in the importance of himself than in that of the tall tale for its own sake; Hazel and Bruce similarly pursue not the betterment of themselves so much as the betterment of their record. And the *true* fools I've encountered are boring in on themselves with central, self-important purpose: the Orphan. Hoop. And my friend Tom, I think, despite his cartoonish surface, somewhere deep took things too seriously and today sounds as if he is not happy. What to make of this? Don't know. Where does, say, Dr. Eminence in Love with Polanski fit in? She is a function of ambition and purpose plotted against achievement and I think will wind up unhappy. Ebert, robbed of central seriousness by racial predicament, will wind up scatterbrained and scatterhearted enough to be happy. James, the factotum, has already comprehended the beauty of failure, the glory of the fancy end run around importance. Does this make sense? Probably it does not. These are lab notes of life by dilettante, not Nobel remarks.

These terms are not right—singularity, towardness, centrality of purpose, self-importance. I am not on it yet. Perhaps I am not citing all the data points. The

Veteran: high singularity of purpose—to locate the dead nigger—but that center is not his by election; it is more correctly his by choice of the United States government, agent *par excellence* of self-important aggrandizement. The Veteran himself we can suspect of having been once not a fool. Am I talking about a quality of oneness of enterprise, one-faceted living?

A simple laid-back vs. square orientation? It seems better expressed somehow else, yet I will confess that the matter does in some senses appear to be one of terms like these. And it may be that the successful operators in this scattered mode are examples simply of lassitude and want of ambition. Still, I want to dignify the downward with another parameter: Are they capitalizing upon liabilities while the others are insisting on investing in assets only? Mary seems able to accept a loss with a victory; Friedeman surely paid for pausing in his career to ponder salvation and damnation; but my own old man preaches pure profit until blue in the face, and I have added to his congestion by simple indifference, which indifference registers for him as aggressive courting of another Depression. Perhaps it is *indifference* which the true fools lack. I cannot say. I will continue to record.

※ / **W**e did towns. Quincy, Panacea, Sopchoppy, Carrabelle, Blountstown—the best town names in the world. We even tried to take a tour of Chattahoochee, the largest state asylum. We'd try something like that and never think of something like Disney World. It became perfectly and agreeably clear that neither of us had any idea what to do. We watched folk who did have ideas.

Cars from Pennsylvania headed south could blow even Mary off the road. Blacks hauling scrap cardboard or cans tooled all over the state at 30, tops. Teenagers in 4 x 4 trucks with tires so large deer could run under the trucks hummed by. And some folks had not so much an idea of what to do as slightly less ignorance about what to do than we did; Florida bars are alive in the mornings. I felt we wrote the book on having a clean slate of purpose.

We spent a day in the town of Branford. The famous Suwannee slugged by in a slow roll to the Gulf, the dark, heavy water cut deep into limestone banks forming moonish, pocked bluffs.

We took a room in a place called *Hotel* that had no desk, no desk clerk, no keys, no locks on doors. Rooms were open for a kind of self-registering. The procedure was to sleep and pay later.

The rooms had screen doors in use, the solid doors behind them left open. White towels were suspended at eye level inside the screen doors for privacy. The door locks were hook latches. A bulb from the ceiling lit the room, controlled by a string to the headboard. The wallpaper had long, rust-colored water stains.

We could hear the other roomers grunt and groan and shuffle around, and one of them fell hard in the night. The mattress was very high on old springs, and we swayed back and forth if either of us turned, rolled together to the soft middle. Mary looked beautiful coming out of the community bathroom with her shiny-washed face early in the morning. We left three dollars on the bed.

We crossed the silver-colored iron bridge over the Suwannee, heading out of town with two large steaming coffees. The river was fogged in: a white, chilled valley.

In odd, hilled towns we found retired whites coming and going around pharmacies that still had soda fountains, and outside these towns, coming and going in

school buses, migrants working orange groves. We
walked into groves to watch the picking. We were never
questioned. We may have looked like a welfare team,
reporters, a landed woman and her heir, I do not know.
We would look at the workers from the edge of the action; the workers at us from cherry pickers, trucks, pallets
of fruit. Mary, wearing a sweater cape-style, would walk
on after a spell, as if the operations were satisfactory.
I followed, a young man pulled for these inspections
from a golf course.

We drank screwdrivers for two days after the first
of these visits, toasting the plight of the poor, and then
we could not stand them anymore and went back to
good, sour tonics.

In one grove we walked up on a hognose snake. I
surprised Mary by picking it up in the middle of its
cobra act. I showed her the snake's small upturned nose
for shoveling out toads from their shallow beds. She
stood about ten feet away—eight feet too far to see the
nose architecture—and said, "Fascinating."

"I was a fool for snakes once," I said. Mary looked
at me as if I'd said the most outlandish thing a man in
a golf suit holding a snake can say to a woman pretending to survey her citrus millions. I put down the hognose, and he instantly performed his death act. I did
not bother to explain.

Somehow we wound up in a hotel bar cuts above
our roadhouse tastes, a well-thought-of old place a little
north of Deerfield Beach. By 11:30 someone at the hotel

had decided we were looking for work there, and we were found uniforms—Mary's a chambermaid affair, mine butler—before the lunch rush. It was a Reuben and tongue crowd. I proclaimed myself no waiter, and the same someone who'd assumed we wanted work said, "No problem." I was told to stand against a wall with a green towel over my arm.

CARLISLE: Mizress Drown to St. Louis, she say for an unpacific number of weeks. We had the sheets already in the barns. Say she would ax that good Reynold buyer to look it *before* market and inside bid and we'd do fine. We did. That's all I got to say. All I know.

And that was Carlisle's total statement in the trial attempting to implicate him in the mulatto-child drowning. A cool fellow. Then his benign and likable cockiness, smoking cigars all over town with his mistress Drown delivering their alleged progeny in St. Louis. I stood against the wall with the green towel on my arm realizing that Carlisle, too, knew how to capitalize on liability, and watched Mary, nearly fluorescent, play the part of a waitress in Florida.

I overheard a table, apparently an employer selling a new applicant on a position with the firm: "All our people are key people. We access you right away to in-house and can interface you after security with on-line for larger work. Compensation packages are just super. And our reputation is one of just super as far as fairness to everyone."

Employee: "My title would be . . .?"

Boss: "Software Specialist. Another?"

Boss orders them more double martinis.

Mary and I leave in late afternoon, walk a fishing pier, and study all the bad luck. It is a spectacular sight to see a school of pompano streak through a disarray of baited lines without touching one: the fishermen standing up, the yellow flares of the fishtails sharp as knives slicing through the lines, the fishermen sitting down.

My friend Tom is part of the world which concerns itself with hot and cold armadillos, and I am not. How did this happen? We were in the same program, the same office, taught the same undergraduates the same chemistry. We appreciated the same scientists. Then he went to Oak Ridge and I went to Bilbo's.

When we pass armadillos, I remark to Mary, "That one looked hot," "That one was cold," and she has no idea what I'm talking about, and does not want to know. Her hair blows madly, whipped thin as cotton candy by the wind.

We are somewhere, now, between social sets: we have done pool halls, open-air bars behind gas stations, and club-sandwich beach clubs. We are presently in a luncheonette vein. Nothing declared, no policy: it is just that two days ago we quit the hotel jobs and have been eating $1.89 lunches in dime stores, served by large, sweaty women who are not unhappy.

Today I have passed another test. It happened that we took a booth next to four hefty women. Mary had her back to them; I faced them, looking over her shoulder. Neither of us took any note—studying the proposition of meat loaf against stuffed pepper—until a trim man with a cane approached them and one of the women said, "The Avon man cometh." She then gave him a playful sock in the arm, and he gave them all a devious smile, sat down, and ordered some coffee. I saw all this, Mary did not, but it was clear to me she heard it: her head was up in a fixed, listening pose, her eyes bright.

The trim man sipped his coffee elegantly and said without self-pity, "I was in Pampers for two months." The women issued noises of mild condolence. "Wearing a diaper is not all bad," the man said, a gleam in his eye. The women seemed satisfied by this remark: they seemed to have an immense respect for him.

One of the women suddenly said, "It *poured* down rain right in the mall parking lot. Before I got inside I was sopping wet, so I went into May Cohen's. They had these blouses for three dollars on a table? I said, I'll take it and change and *wear* it. The one I was wearing was stuck, you know, *to my bra*—" She paused, and the women looked at the man for a moment, during which he did not move or look directly at any woman.

# A Woman
## Named Drown

"Anyway," the woman picked up, "they were marked down from *twenty-three dollars* and I thought I had me a *buy.*"

Another woman felt the material of her sleeve.

"That's the one?" a third woman asked.

"Yes, honey, that's why I'm telling you this." The remaining two women felt the material.

"*Well.* Everything has a gimmick. You won't believe this. Look. This is why it was three dollars."

The woman stood up, moved a distance from their table, and shrugged her shoulders several times, ending in an arms-straight-down posture, standing woodenly and slumped before them. Her sleeves had slipped down six inches past her hands, giving her the aspect of a rayon ape.

"Can you *believe* it?" she said. "Everything has a gimmick."

The other ladies clucked a good-natured disgust. The trim man was stoic, uncommenting, sipping his coffee. The woman had modeled her shirt directly to him, her bra not precisely invisible in this dry blouse.

Mary never turned to witness this scene, but she watched me watch, and I believe that I passed. It is a kind of theater no hack playwright could stage, and I believe that is what she wants me to see in this and in every other mundane adventure we happen to witness.

Mary is getting younger by the day. We are ever more lost to the practical world, more located in our desired universe of self-directed drama.

＊ / **W**e are riding again, Mercury tearing the highway air out of itself. Mary's looking fine in a T-shirt. I'm in one, too. We're up to some kind of redneck act, it seems.

At an interstate picnic rest area, we saw an alligator eating golf balls. A woman was opening the door of an RV and tossing out one golf ball at a time to the alligator. I stood there and watched in my Stump suit. Between tosses a second woman came out of nowhere and started reading me the riot act about endangered species and federal animal-welfare acts and I helplessly protested. She would not believe I had nothing to do with the feeding. "Watch that trailer," I told her. Nothing happened.

I knocked on the RV. A man opened the door. A

hairy gut hung out, which forced his T-shirt to ride up to his chest. "Forget it, pal," he said.

"Forget what?"

"Whatever crap you are." He slammed the door.

I walked back to Mrs. Audubon. "See?" I said.

"I already saw, just like I said," she said.

I return to the consummate logic of flying in the Mercury, mixing drinks in midair, taking life's lab notes. There is no misunderstanding like that golf-ball business between the back seat and front. Mary adjusts the rearview mirror until our eyes meet; she's ordering a light tonic with a lot of lime. She stops the car and freshens up in a rest room, comes out with new lipstick and her hair brushed back: the four-o'clock double, no lime. She drives. I serve drinks to the driver.

About this time I join her in the front, and until dark we are at our touristy best, watching Florida's sandy glare become Florida's neon evening. One of us comes up with something to say, usually by gesture alone, about Chico's Monkey Emporium, Floyd's Go-Cart Royale, a Hep-Ur-Sef station, the Daytona Pamplona (a Cuban disco, we think). A club advertising music by Maurice and the Fucking Parrots is too much: Mary takes her foot off the accelerator as we pass it. We look at each other. The club's marquee actually proclaims: TONIGHT: MAURICE AND THE FUCKING PARROTS.

Maurice and the Fucking Parrots are the worst band you could assemble with human musicians, or parrot musicians, for that matter, and we dance for hours. We rest in the car, watching the clear skies darken, the crushed-shell parking lot begin to whiten with a light of its own, peaceful as the moon. The night is ruined so aggressively, so eagerly, so thoroughly by Maurice's horrible music that it is somehow made perfect.

We rescue ourselves finally at two with the Mercury's powerful rumble and surge into the chilled highway air. Mary throws her head back and to the side, lips parted, silent actress awaiting a kiss. We stop on an undeveloped piece of A1A and walk into some low dunes with Stump's navy blankets.

"Balance the books tomorrow," she says. It is an odd note.

We got up the next morning to a changed world— to a new act, I might should say. I do not know whether to blame—blame is not the word, let's say to hold accountable—Maurice and the Fucking Parrots or not.

We got up, normal as you please, greasy-faced from a night of Atlantic sand and wind, ready for a day-rate room and some rest, and Mary took the stage.

"Al, make a check for two thousand. To yourself."

I am writing today, not in the Mercury, but beside a plywood stand selling key-lime pies. I have eaten two slices of pie to justify writing on a picnic table beside the pie stand, but am drawing suspicious looks all the same. The girl in the stand has a tape player. We have just heard Freddie Fender sing of "wasted days and wasted nights." Now Diana Ross of "no mountain high enough."

We had taken the motel room, showered, and I sat down near the door. Mary sat on the bed, her arms on her knees, leaning toward me like a father. "There's nothing personal in this," she said.

"In what?"

"You can take the Merc or the two thousand."

I looked at her, and the color TV, on a stand about eye level with me. I mulled this one over until I found myself playing with my lips and stopped.

"I understand," I said. What was odd was that I believe I did understand. She was closing a very successful road show and meant for us, as actors, to move on. And she was clever enough to fold following a packed-house night rather than when the play was in trouble.

"What about Stump's wardrobe?" I said.

"I'll take it if you want a new one."

I pictured myself in the clothes I would get from the nearest Stuckey's—monkey T-shirts treated with Tris, orange surfing trunks coming to my knees—and said I'd keep Stump's if it was all right. It was more unnatural, in her scheme of things, for her to reclaim her husband's tattered clothes than for me to simply wear them out.

"Okay." She got up and signed a check and came

over to me and bent at the waist and rolled her forehead across mine, back and forth, holding my neck, like inking a thumb for fingerprints, and walked out the door with a jangle of keys, a swift solid car door, a blast, a reverse, a small rock skid, gentle rubbery crushing of stone.

The check for two thousand dollars was beside the ice bucket. I kept the door open, letting natural light in, while I showered again and watched TV and otherwise took advantage of the room until checkout. I expected to feel abandoned or lonely, but I did not, exactly. I felt I had observed the terms of our dramatic no-bio creed and was a fine performer and had no call to long for anything under the sun. And it still hurt, some.

Adjacent to the motel was the key-lime pie stand, looking like four plywood Ping-Pong tables thrown into an A-frame, housing a pasty-faced girl you might see at a trailer park. I ate the two slices of pie at a picnic table and looked at the highway.

❦ / **A** bus came along and let a load of tourists have at the key-lime pie stand, and I got on. Heading west, through what I think was once Everglades, we passed a HELP WANTED sign and I got off. I walked down a white graded road to a fish camp.

The building was small and low, suggesting an enclosed trailer. It had plywood floors and a plywood ceiling, about head high. Down the longest reach of the joint a woman was throwing darts. She was not throwing them at a dart board and she was not throwing them with the deft, wristy, English toss. She was letting them go like Bob Feller, lead leg higher than her head. On the wall forty feet away was a target painted in crude circles. The bull's-eye alone was big as a bowling ball.

When she finished up the set, I said, "Is there a job here?"

"Ho!" she said, plucking the darts loose. She went behind the bar. She got a beer and slid it to me and took one herself. She broke her pop top without opening the beer, and holding a dart dagger-style, she neatly collapsed the tab with one punch.

"These things changed my world," she said. She flicked the ring off the bar to the floor.

I nodded. I looked out the door, to the water. There was a fallen dock, and tied to it some wooden rowboats sunk to gunwales. They looked like alligators.

"So," she said. "Drink all you want, eat if you want to, don't give any customers a hard time."

"That's it?"

She didn't answer, except to wipe the bar with a ribbed towel which she flopped around like leavening bread. Certain parallels—equivalences were I in a lab instead of a fish camp, in a true reaction series rather than life's—were stunning. Instead of a pool shark, before me stood some kind of major-league dart pitcher. Where there had been gin, there was beer. And it looked as though the same no-questions, no-lies ambience was going to operate.

I suddenly saw that Mary had truly acted according to the constants and coefficients and activities and affinities of the whole series of reactions around me defining this odd interlude. She "left me" with no more

wrongful or sorrowful moment than an atom leaves
another, than blood becomes iron and oxygen. And I
was the evolving product, now in a fish-camp retort
with a new reagent not unlike—in fact, startlingly
similar to—the last. Who governed these combinations?
How could it all be a random walk?

Down near the water was a large kid. He got in
one of the sunken boats and started bailing with a cut-
out Clorox-bottle scoop tied to his wrist.

"Do we rent those boats to customers?"

She had arranged the darts into a neat parallel
arsenal on the bar and lit a cigarette and sat up close
on the other side on a stool. She put her beer on a cardboard coaster and passed me one.

"If somebody ever wants a boat, mister, you take
their money and drive to Sears and make the down
payment on a johnboat. Then, if somebody *else* wants
one, we'll rent a boat." She took a giant drag on her
cigarette, blowing smoke to the ceiling, in a spreading
roil.

At the boats, the kid was bailing away.

"Or let Bonaparte go to Sears," she said. "That kid
can *drive*." She leaned a bit to one side and got a look
of concentration on her face. I thought she was straining to see Bonaparte. I heard an odd, small, mewing
noise. "Hope you don't mind gas," she said.

"It's two things he does. Drive and bail. It would
be *Christmas* if he got to drive *and* get a dry boat."

Bonaparte was sitting almost chest deep, scooping the water near him and pouring it out at arm's length.

"Bonaparte," I said.

"That might be cruel," she said. "That might be cruel." She threw the ribbed rag at a big sink behind the bar.

"They told me he had a bone apart in his head to explain his condition. That's how they said it, too. Well, we weren't too excited about it. We weren't too excited about it and got drunk, and next thing we're calling him Bonaparte. Is that cruel?"

"I don't know," I said.

"You ready?"

Before I could gesture, another beer slid to within an inch of the one I was on. Bonaparte, steadily working, seemed to pause and listen to something between pours of his scoop. He was not more than a head and an arm bailing in a blinding disk of sun on water.

"He gives me the *vim* to go on," she said. I noticed him again pause as if listening to distant signals.

"So, where'd you leave your clubs, Arnie?" She laughed at herself.

"Let's get you some khakis and tell all the customers you're the fish guide. Can you see the expression on their face when you wade into one of them wrecks with a Lorance under your arm?" She started wheezing with laughter. Recovering, she said, "That *is* some suit."

We drank, looking at Bonaparte bail.

"You wasn't . . . *golfing*, was you?"

"No," I said.

"You a darts man?"

"Might be."

She marched over, lined up, wound up, and delivered—the dart went a half inch into the wall with a gratifying *thuuung*. On my turn, I missed the whole target, but I hit the wall and I hit it very hard, and she watched me like a spring-training scout, arms folded. "You catch on fast," she said.

We played a game. In the late going—innings, I guess—she'd actually paw the floor as if grooving the mound, and *grunt* when she released. I had never seen better form. Not a customer came.

The fish-camp position made my time at Mary's seem an apprenticeship. Or it may be that Mary had me so well trained that certain early mistakes were avoided at the camp. Her name was Wallace ("That's cruel, too. Don't call me Wally"), she played no roles other than the main one, and I mistook her for none else. You don't see a woman like her in a Sunday supplement. I did see her frequently in the regional fishing weekly, *The Glade Wader*. She'd create accounts of boatloads of fish brought in at our nameless camp (in the paper she called us Bonaparte's) and phone this apocrypha in to the editor, when we had not even made the down payment on the johnboat and Bonaparte was flailing away harder than ever.

We would clean the place—it never got messed up, really, but we soaked it down in Pine-Sol in the mornings anyway, because the cats carried crabs and fish under it and we were in effect disinfecting the ground as well as the floors. We poured gallons of pine-smelling ammonia out and swabbed ourselves into sweats by ten in the morning and split a six-pack and looked out of the easy gloom of the bar into the headachy light, and there, committed as a saint, full of belief, bailing the entire Gulf of Mexico, was Bonaparte. He took to blowing a whistle periodically, perhaps designating invisible progress.

"*Vim*," Wallace would say, both of us squinting at Bonaparte, both of us nodding, happy to be inside, in the cool gloom, dizzy on fumes and cold carbonation. A man came in one afternoon, sized the place up, had a beer, listened to Bonaparte bail and whistle, said, "Sounds like a disco out there," and left.

A couple came in one morning and watched him bail for a while before suddenly going into a disquisition on hippies. "We saw a van," the man said. "Purple."

"With *butterflies* on it," the woman added.

"All *over* it," the man said.

Wallace served them. We were just finishing the Pine-Sol detail. The woman opened both their beers and poured them into glasses which she inspected in the light before filling, squinting her nose at the ammonia. We could hear Bonaparte working as steadily in the glare coming from outside as a pump in an oilfield.

The light came in whole and hot and salty, and reflected off the damp board floor in broken, mirrory planes. The customers were shading their eyes.

"I wish all I had to do was drive around in a dope van all day," the man said.

"With *butterflies* on it," added the woman.

"That would be *the life*." He motioned to Wallace for beer number two. It was 10:30.

"Hippies," the woman said.

"What's he *doing* out there?" the man asked, with an emphasis that somehow seemed to link Bonaparte with the hippies.

"He's bailing, you sonofabitch," Wallace said, and she walked to the dart wall and planted a foot up on it and yanked out a dart. She wound up and fired one, and the sonofabitch and his wife left.

"See what I mean about you not offending customers?" she asked me. "*I* can do it, and I can do *enough* of it."

She fired three darts. "Sonofabitch thinks he can drink beer at ten o'clock and some kid can't drive a purple truck." A three-legged cat walked in with a large live crab in its mouth. "Get outside, honey," she said to it, and the cat backed easily out, the crab waving claws to us, as if for help.

After the demonstration of Wallace's diplomacy with customers, I assumed a new demeanor around the few that straggled in. I was a kind of personal valet, the ambassador of good will at Bonaparte's. My job, as

I saw it, was to prevent customers from talking, lest they draw Wallace's wrath. I usually took their beer orders with the gravity of a funeral-home operator, giving a long, soulful look directly at them, then the slightest, tenderest nod I could manage toward Bonaparte out at the docks, then another kind of nod toward Wallace. This Wallace nod was in the thumb-jerk category, but was very subdued, and I followed it with a shrug, as if to say, *Given the kid out there, the lady is disturbed, and likely to go off, you understand.* Most did—in fact, some customers, provided this one-two of tactful apprising, gave an exaggerated and solemn nod of their own, clammed up altogether, and would *point* to their brand of beer rather than call it. These folk I had where I wanted—I felt like a matador with the bull quieted and sword ready. Wallace would interrupt the moment of their reverential silence with a great, sudden *thuuung* of dart that would make them spill beer.

Much of the beer consumed was consumed by Wallace and me. We got into a game of drinking certain kinds to correspond with brand deliveries, turning off all the beer clocks and signs except those representing the day's brand. We looked like seven individual low-budget beer commercials. I got inordinately fond of the first beers in the morning that we used to slake through the Pine-Sol, which felt like it was in our throats and *was* in our heads. The clear, cold bubbles of the beer washed in, *stinging* through the piney, gaggy, cottonlike ammoniac air of the freshly mopped bar, and after a good hard mopping that made you sweat and a couple of good cold cold ones to clear the eyes, we'd struggle to the wide, bright door and look out at pure air and heat and Bonaparte bailing and the headachy convection currents already coming off his toiling form and feel, somehow—I did, and I think Wallace did, too—as if the day was wonderful, the place fine, the weather clear, the salt tonic, the world good.

Across this happy-face moment would then waft a small cloud of the real, and we'd step back abruptly and get another beer and realize we were broke, Bonaparte was hopeless, and the sole rescue was hundreds of customers who wanted boats we did not have, fish no one could show them to, hospitality we were fundamentally opposed to granting. Then we'd have a fourth beer, and then it was, well before noon, altogether too bright to look at Bonaparte for any longer than you'd look directly at the sun itself if someone told you it was in lunar eclipse. I would prepare myself for the unlikely advent of customers by placing on my arm an imaginary green towel of the sort I'd worn when Mary and I worked at the beach club.

It was in all a wonderful time that I knew even during the nose-pinching smallness of it I would remember as fondly as you remember certain mean periods of your life and come to love them for the meanness. Wallace I respected as a soldier—a person who would have gone to West Point and been a rogue general who, despite a career of insubordination, *won*; or a middling prizefighter who won on indomitability alone. Instead, she had a bone-apart child and a fishless fish camp and bottomless boats and won by strategic, stubborn refusal to accede to . . . to what? I did not know: I do not know. She refused to ask for any *relief*—it was as if what she wanted was not a break but one more trial: one more dart in the plywood of her ordeal. And that dart she wanted implanted, solidly, stuck into the heart of the whole losing proposition.

I could not even figure, while I ate it, where the bologna we had for lunch came from. The meat may have been in the chest freezer that Bonaparte froze his crabs in. I never looked in it, because the one time I thought to, it was slept upon by a placid cat with one dusty eyeball goggling out, actually touching the rusty top of the freezer. I saw no cause to wake him. You don't disturb a cat like that to see bologna.

Performing my silent duties as valet to the nearly hypothetical customer, I got to feeling that while Wallace might be set up for the next dart of oppression, I was not, and I hardly saw how my not scaring a couple of couples before they had two beers each could possibly equal my consuming nearly as much bologna as Bonaparte—he was *voracious*—and I decided to get out before the next dark dart struck. In fact, it occurred to me that *I had been it*—the next dart—when I arrived. And now we all awaited the next profitless windfall. These were the events that Bonaparte tracked, perhaps, with his head cockings and whistlings and St. Vitusing out under the broken green-shaded light at the end of the dock.

"Wallace, write me a check for fifteen hundred dollars and I'll give you one for two thousand and you can get him a boat. I'm going."

She turned to me, sucking the finger she burned turning the rising mounds of bologna. Bonaparte did not like punctures. "What?"

"Sambo rumbles."

"Kiss my ass."

She turned back to the stove. I got my grocery bag of Stump's duds and left, passing Bonaparte in the marsh checking his crab traps.

At the end of the white, graded road where I'd gotten off the bus, nothing had changed, which somehow surprised me. I expected to see even the same bus come barreling down on me from the same direction I had ridden it. I was stunned to be standing where I had stood, and exactly *as* I had stood before, except for the passage of time at the camp, as if I were a boat sunk to my nose and bailing myself out with all the efficacy of Bonaparte up to his chin. You can feel odd standing in a sudden swarm of deerflies—having just thrown darts for a month with a woman you've left with her retarded kid—rippling sawgrass as far as the eye can see, razory salty wheat.

Air brakes caught me dreaming. Before me *was* the same bus, the same driver. I got on. He smiled at me as if I were a traveling salesman returning from a joke. I offered a hundred-dollar bill for the fare and took the smirk off his face.

"Napoleon musta got one dry," he said, expecting me to share with him the lunacy of my days at the camp. I did not. I heard a faint, shrill whistle from behind the bus as we were getting going. Wallace was nailing up the HELP WANTED sign and Bonaparte was whistling and listening vigorously. Then, from too far to tell for sure, I swear he dropped trou and mooned the bus. The driver was looking in his side mirror, but his expression gave no clue.

In Naples I got heroic. I paid for Sears' top-of-the-line johnboat and had it delivered. And I got it in my head to go home.

✿ / How ow so nutty a notion took hold of me I can only guess. Throwing darts through Pine-Sol fumes or reading amateur playscripts for a living sets you up for a broadsiding by any crack-brained thing that comes along remotely redolent of the practical or normal or responsible, I suppose. And so I decided to go home, and I also decided to impress the bus driver by writing as we flew up the backside of Florida. I acquired another notebook from a newsstand in a bus station, and I carried it past the driver with a processional gravity, as if I were a priest. I am still in a kind of cold war with the bus driver.

I have written on a wire table, in a Mercury, at an ammoniac fish camp, and now on a Big Red bus out of Naples, Florida, barreling up the murky coast of Florida, going to see my old man. He and my mother live in

Lafayette in a mansion. There will be liquor, and insults regarding my not taking over the oil-field-supply business.

It is impossible to believe that whatever Mary trained me for, or whatever I sought the day I broke rank, is coming to a visit with my old man. Nothing is less agreeable.

I'd better rethink this whole business. I'm now in the position, after all, of *missing connections*. It is easy to stop in Tallahassee, take too long walking to see the capitol dome, miss the bus for Mobile, and take the one for Quitman.

Show up in Quitman and start from there. Nothing is easier, or harder, than that.

My second day a-bus. Certain things are becoming clear. At 10:30 this morning in Chipley, Florida, I entered a Suwannee Swifty and bought a red T-shirt, a large Big Red soda water, and resumed my seat directly over the bus-side exhortation to GO BIG RED. This theater made me the envy of two children who got on the bus, to whom I gave the soft drink. It worked: I "became someone" through a maneuver of artificial staging. I need more funky shirts, more improbable women, more nerve. We head south, to the Gulf, non-express.

Carrabelle flies by in a town-sized convection current.

The red shirt stinks of cheap dye.

The bus glides.

The girl who got on at Niceville I tell I'm a song-writer, and my new song, "I'm Happy to Be the One That's Mostly on Top of You," I'm going to dedicate to her.

"Say *whut*?"

The bus has taken an unexpected stop—for a flat, being attended to now by a Montgomery Ward truck—in Panacea. I enter Eastside Beverage. A white man is saying to a black named Augusta (from his work-shirt embroidery), "He is a nice snake." Augusta says, "Don't start on me that shit." "I'll show you," the proprietor says, heading for the back. Augusta gets off his stool, ready to run, full of mock fear and a little true fear.

The proprietor returns with a cigar box, opens it: a boxful of snapshots.

"Oh," Augusta says. "All right."

In a photo the white man holds a large diamond-back in one smooth loop between its head and tail. The mouth is open, slack. "We enjoyed each other," the proprietor says. Augusta looks at him with quick, hard, mock disapproval and some real disapproval. Apparently the proprietor is seeking to have Augusta believe the snake was alive and his pet.

"That's a dead snake," I say.

"Yeah, he died."

"No, he's dead right there."

The proprietor does some sizing up of me. I get two quarts of beer I do not want, to remain casual and fluid.

"That snake was dead before you ever got *near* it."

Augusta studies the picture.

"These two quarts of beer are for Augusta, a man who knows bullshit."

Augusta says, "That I do." He looks at the proprietor in a way designed, however, to let him know he thinks I'm crazy.

I'm on the bus. I've hit on something. I may be nuts, feebleminded, but I've run agreeably aground on something.

When my degree at Tennessee is conferred or not, when James has forgotten my room of stuff, the carp my symbolic lock, Ebert his basketball, Camel Tent the collegiate new girl, Mary our quaint ride, Wallace my kiss-ass leave, I will be remembered along here as the guy who said Floyd Drowdy's alleged pet rattlesnake was a dead fake, and Augusta will take less shit and do less jiving around that rotten-tooth white simp than before, and every day he walks in there and says, Let me have a look at that *pet*, the role I played will continue to be remembered.

We get back up out of this coast-run hernia and head true west—on the same road Mary and I took, I think, U.S. 90—we stop at a gas station. I'm *amazed*: it's the one where Mary and I stopped, behind which

Bobby Cherry and the geezers talked of owls. I look behind it. Everybody's there. I wave. They look at me. Then a look of recognition. Cherry is the first to dis-acknowledge this, by looking down at his own beer, so I sit at his table, where I sat before.

"Bobby."

"Sport."

After a beer, in utter silence, I lean over to him. "Are you the kind of guy *does* what he *says* he's going to do?"

"What?"

"You heard me."

"Get him a beer." Bobby Cherry points to me. A geezer in an apron goes to the cooler.

"I take it that's important, still. The *word*."

"Damn straight."

"And you're *that kind*."

"Damn straight."

"Good."

Bobby Cherry's getting concerned. "Why is it good?" he says.

"I want you to be the kind of guy you say you are."

"You don't think I am?"

"Didn't say that."

"I better get in my truck before I do something I regret."

"Get in your truck."

He does. Easy as that.

. . .

In a dime store in Milton, Florida, I tell the clerk, "I don't *think* I'm a Communist."

She passes my items past her: a balsa glider in a flat pack, tube socks, a tin box of split shot.

"I *know* you're not a Communist," she says. "I wish it would rain."

"Yes, ma'am. I know you do. It's a shame we undid the Indians," I say. "They had those rain dances. Marched about a million of them right by here on the way to Oklahoma, too."

"Nope," she says, sacking my airplane, socks, shot.

"No?"

"Trucked 'em. Wouldn't let 'em touch the ground."

"Shame."

"Pity."

"We are bad."

She looks at me. I am testing her now.

"We are *bad*," I say again. "You have hundreds of rubber buffalo and Indians in here for sale." Perhaps she will think I'm a Communist, after all.

It is the old kind of dime store: brass nails are worn up through the pine floors, large white opaque global lights hang from the ceiling. Nothing of any value can be seen on the shelves, in the bins. Yet several poor-looking women feel things, load them, buy them—orange plastic toys, nylon hose, clothes pins, perfume. The soda fountain is intact, closed. No public-address voice will ever exhort shoppers to pay attention to anything in here. No yellow light will be wheeled around to sale zones. As a consequence, everyone pays attention to everything, regards everything as a sale item. I have narrowly avoided purchasing a menagerie of small rubber monsters, after feeling them for minutes, watching for the bus driver, who I think has started nipping. He is clever. He disappears for a few minutes at these endless country stops, where there is rarely a formal bus station. I believe he would leave me if he could. Our cold war is strong.

I have begun distributing gifts to children on the bus, for which he doubtless thinks me a pederast. I get back on and whisper to the driver, "I'm an existentialist, pure and simple." He says nothing.

In Fairhope I follow him, catch him in the men's room pulling on a half pint of Seagram's. "You're an existentialist, too," I say, washing up.

"I'm a drunk, kid." He says this with no emphasis— no confession, no self-pity. I offer to shake hands. We have a good, firm, countryman's shake.

"When the hell is this ride over?"

"Mobile."

"Not New Orleans?"

"Not me."

"It's been a good one."

He is taking another tight-lipped shot, which he sucks in with a teeth-baring grimace. He cants the bottle to me. I roll a long slug in, open-throated, careful not to lip his bottle. We exit together, I get the door and he touches my shoulder in return.

It *has* been a good bus ride. Now the driver and I are on even terms: I am above the common passenger, he is lower than ship's captain. In Mobile, end of the line, we run into each other at the same run-down hotel where he stays regularly. "Lot of Greek in this town," he says in the lobby. He is out of uniform. In a flowered shirt, he suddenly looks seedy, dangerous.

"Are you Greek?" I ask.

"*Hell* no." He laughs. "I *eat* Greek. Plenty Greek to eat here."

We wind up in the Athens Bar & Grill, where a woman in green chiffon is trying to smother seated gentlemen with her breasts while undulating her fatty navel at them. After a couple of bottles of retsina, we eat something. The dancing gets wilder. Fatima-Helen retires and middle-aged Greek men take over. They make mime breasts, sculpt them out of air, and tease one another with them. They hunch one another. One falls on his knees, miming sucking his partner.

"Shall we have more turpentine?" I ask.

"I've had enough."

"You must *not* be Greek."

"I'm normal. I drive that bus twelve years. My wife has cancer. My son works for the highway department. My wife will die."

"I'm sorry."

"They're burning her now. They're in that stage. This is not a joke. She stays *hot*."

"I'm sorry."

"Don't mention it."

We watch the show, the men dancing, their own wives watching them perform these suggestions.

I suddenly know I am going back to Knoxville.

"These Greeks are sports, aren't they?" I say.

He—the driver, we have not exchanged names—shakes his head, agreeably, sadly, gets up to go.

In the hotel corridor the next morning I pass two black women eating bagels. They are in custodial blues, sitting heavily in a supply room, watching a fire-alarm light blinking on the wall.

"Is the building afire?" I ask.

One of the women says, "The buzzer ain't gone off."

We look at the light, blinking regularly, fast. "I thought it smelled like fire in here *last night*," I say. "It stank."

"Yes, it did," the second woman says. She is farther into the janitor's closet, not eating. She has a bagel with a neatly applied quarter inch of butter troweled onto it. It is as if she will not begin eating until the message carried by the blinking light is understood.

"Well," I say, "I'm checking *out*."

They laugh, nodding.

"I love you," I say to them.

The second one, with the ready bagel, says, "You *say* that."

"I say that."

The first woman looks at me, looks away.

It seems to me that people are ready to hear things never heard before so long as they are not frightened for their physical safety or worried that listening may cost them money. This is an untestable hypothesis, and I don't know that I want to test it now that I have formed the hypothesis so neatly. But I believe I gave it a fair test for a few days, and proved it sufficiently well for a failed scientist. People are hungry for new utterance. Does the reaction series of life include new utterance in its function?

Can Mary be said to have shown me this by assuming roles and living them? Was Bonaparte receiving and sending wavelengths so novel no one in his right mind could pick up on them?

✺ / In the cafeteria of the bus station I saw my driver again, dressed for the road, looking invisible and harmless, in his blue regulation suit. He poured a saucerful of coffee back into his cup, the saucer shaking at a frequency so high and an amplitude so low that anyone unconscious of wave theory would not have seen it shake. His whole attitude suggested a man holding his breath. I joined him.

"Back to Florida?" I asked him.

"Shoot. A run north. Little-town run. From Decatur over to Jackson."

"From where?"

"Decatur."

"I know someone there."

I got up to get us more coffee and to check behind the counter for Rod Serling: crackerjack nuke-whiz

Tom lived in Decatur, Alabama. The plottable slope of fate defining my errant life was running straight to Tom.

"I know someone there I'd like to see."

"Well, come on. I'll take you there." He said this as if he meant in his own car, at his own expense, and he sort of did. He told me to meet him in seventeen minutes three blocks down the street and he'd pick me up.

"Sync up," he said, exposing his wristwatch in a flourish of his uniformed arm. We matched our watches like spies. All of this was to save me a six-dollar ticket.

"I fucked some turkeys there when I was a kid," he said.

"You what?"

"Fucked turkeys."

"Fucked *turkeys*?"

"Yeah. I was staying with my cousin and he asked if I wanted to fuck something, so I said sure, and he showed me these turkeys he said his father didn't want, and we fucked them."

"What do you mean, *didn't want*?"

"Well, it kills 'em, you know."

"Kills 'em."

"Kills hell out of 'em, actually." He grinned a not altogether ashamed grin.

"Only my uncle *did* want them. Beat the hell out of us."

In our remaining time he gave me a short course

in bestiality. Cows one does barefoot, holding the
Achilles tendon with the big toe. Sheep with their hind
legs in your Wellies.

"Dogs?"

"Never fucked a dog."

This seemed an oversight to me.

"Did fuck some bass once."

I looked at him. Was he on to the theory of new
utterance himself? Was he just doing some Sweetlips
pygmy on me? I thought maybe he was not. He was
too somber at some level to be kidding.

"Bass," I said. "How in hell do you fuck bass?"

"In the"—he pointed down his throat—"the little
muscle thing there." He meant the fluted, sphincterlike
throat, and it had an aptness so thorough I did not
doubt him. I was talking to a sad, alcoholic bus driver
who had fucked bass as a kid. I was talking to a natural
in the world of folk who can celebrate their liabilities,
carry their failures.

"I've got a friend up in Decatur who hunts armadillos for radiation exposure," I said. "Maybe you
can—"

"Radiation's a sore point with me, bud."

On the way to Decatur he told me of his wife's
travail, a not atypical one, I presume. Her life had been
prolonged by radiation, he supposed, but watching
her suffer, he did not see the point of it. She was hair-
less, incontinent, and, as he put it, hot. At night he held

her hand. He did not mind being on the road now. He applied, in fact, for long, errant tours of duty taking him anywhere but home.

He drove me to Tom's very door, where I debarked in a great hydraulic hiss onto a neatly trimmed yard in a new suburb. Tom came out grinning like an idiot, appreciating the joke of my being delivered, a lone passenger, by so large a vehicle, to his otherwise undistinguished residence. The driver and I shook hands. He declined to come in. He eased the giant machine around the corner and slowly out of sight.

❦ / The drop-in is not all it was once in the South, and my timing in coming to see Tom was not good. Tom and his wife, Elaine, were expecting guests for the weekend—the twin girls of Elaine's sister. At first I thought that crowding alone was to be the principal hitch, but things got complex.

When the girls arrived, Elaine fawned over them in a demonstrative way I suspect was calculated to show Tom something, and I came to think the something was that they needed girls, or children, *just like these*. Tom entertained them with nervous cartoonisms, affecting a kind of Dr. Seuss character. Elaine acted happily dazed, serving as a kind of buffer between Tom and the somber girls, who, as if in opposition, were mature and smiled only when obligated.

After dinner the girls were put to bed and we sat talking. Tom got a brilliant light in his eyes and said to me, "Do you know what Elaine does?"

"I do not," I reported.

Elaine gravely started to peel her blouse over her head. I wondered if I had badly misjudged them. Beneath her blouse was a T-shirt proclaiming *Slingshot champ of 1249 Bowick.*

Tom leaped from the table, returning with a cardboard box, in the bottom of which was a carpet sample. It was one of our targets before we got the tents and the rats. Elaine was flexing the surgical tubing of a slingshot, inspecting for fissures. "Tom had this made at the shop at work. Aircraft aluminum." I had my first look at a nuclear-reactor slingshot.

For an hour we shot into the box Tom's array of suburban grapeshot: marbles, slugs, rocks, fishing weights, ball bearings, a wild thing that looked like a lead pecan cluster.

"This should be in the Olympics," Tom said.

"Are there any rats?" I asked.

"Rats?" Tom asked, as if he had forgotten our previous time with the slingshot. "No. No rats. None in town." There was a momentary drop in Tom's goofy mirth, a kind of amnesiac stare I was not familiar with.

"Tom," Elaine said.

It was not clear what had happened, what Elaine meant, what Tom had provoked. Tom put the box con-

taining all the grapeshot away. Elaine showed me a
guest room, appointed in all details, towels to alarm
clock, and retired. I got the entirely unsupportable
impression that she was wondering what Tom had ever
seen in me and felt, so accused, that I couldn't blame
her.

Tom and I stayed up in the kitchen. I had given no
explanation for my arrival and had expected to have to—
Tom was usually downright nosy about school and how
well or badly folk were doing. *Flunked out* was a phrase
he liked to repeat until it was ludicrous. Telling him I
quit Friedeman would ordinarily produce his largest
ear-to-ear, incredulous smile. But he was not curious.
We sat and listened to Elaine closing doors.

Tom looked down the hall. I thought of our once
having wadded up my tent out on the fire escape and
firing the slingshot down the long reach of the apartment hall past the Orphan's and Veteran's doors, prepared to tell anyone who challenged us we were
humoring the Veteran with a dead fucking nigger can-
non. I thought Tom was just possibly calculating for a
long-hall setup. He remained still.

"Tom, no *rats*?"

"Paul White tapirs?" The old glee. Paul White was
our landlord. "Are tapirs really *rodents*? How could
they be? I'd like to see the *teeth*." This was the old
Tom.

"I can't *imagine* rodents that large," I said.

"Me either."

He studied the hall. "No rats." Again I thought I saw a change, a little dark flash.

I got up and got a GO BIG RED commemorative half-pint out of my bag. To my surprise Tom did not decline it. He is legendary for sustained and exclusive consumption of soft drinks.

"They take those kids to live filmings of *Sesame Street*," he said. "Make them listen to NPR. Had their birthday announced from Lake Wobegon. No nitrates. No *cereal*."

I recalled his card to me:

*Remember Elaine? (Good girl.) I married her. Sold tent. Sold Mustang. It was a good car.*

And then enthusiasm about a "ghoul mouse," as I recall.

We sat there, listening to appliances and other subtle noises of a house settling for the night, passing the half-pint. I told Tom about the kid chopping onions who couldn't take it. I told him about all the fools I'd seen who were smarter than you'd think because they were not letting their lives become constructs of what was expected of them. I felt like the polyester preacher and shut up. I'm not sure Tom understood me, and I'm certain that wasn't his fault. Perhaps I wasn't even speaking to the central causes of his depression. But it *looked* like he wasn't all fired up about living the life good-girl Elaine had cooked up for them.

We heard one more firm door closing in the back of the house, a final not loud sound that somehow communicates lost patience on the part of those going to bed with those not. It didn't look like any fun to me. I thought of all the careless fun I'd been having with women who offered no closing-door crap, of old Dr. Eminence in Love with Polanski, who had presumably set this whole reaction series to rolling.

"You still going to Norway?" Tom asked. It was frankly unbelievable—as if we were thought-for-thought with each other.

"No. As they say in Brooklyn, das out."

"Sort of thought so."

"Why?"

"It never was going to work."

"Why not?"

"Don't know." He probably thought he did, but wasn't going to speculate. I think we were both coming to the conclusion that we didn't know each other at all beyond the slingshot lunacy.

"What about you?" I said.

"What?"

"You and—"

"It'll work."

"How do you know?"

"I'll make it."

"You'll make it or you'll make it work?"

"Make it work."

"You'd better get an extra bedroom for Fenster."

"Or an *extra house!*" Like that, he was restored, grinning openly at the prospect of Fenster's alter-life beside his, I suppose. I'm sure he could see getting Fenster's lights turned on, getting his credit established. Fenster could shoot his slingshot late at night. Fenster would have rats. Fenster Ludge would raise *tapirs*.

In the reaction-series-of-life scheme of things, Fenster would care for his untowardness as much as for his self-actualizing assets and towardness. Fenster could take a step backward or to the side now and again. Fenster Ludge would be a dallying kind of dude.

Tom got up and left the room and returned with a giant trophy that had a tiny car on its top. He set it on the table.

"I won the Soap Box Derby," he said.

"Come on."

"For years I thought I was sliced bread."

I looked at the trophy. Something about it looked real. He *had* won the damned Soap Box Derby.

"My God, son."

"The Soap Box Derby is nothing but going downhill with amateurs." Tom intoned this with a note of bitterness that convinced me I did not know him at all.

"What the hell is it *supposed* to be, Tom?"

"No, the thing is—" He made a gesture in the air, as if to indicate the entire environs—walls, wife, nieces, the stars above.

"Okay, Tom."

Sometime in the night I got up and ran into Elaine coming out of the bathroom. We did one of those side-to-side unsuccessful evasions people do in the same path—she did not smile. She looked down, holding her robe at the throat, and finally passed. Again I got the impression she was in thorough contempt of me, though, in fact, she was simply a tired woman in a bathrobe trying to get by a strange man in her house at 3 a.m. The sensation of her disapproval was strong enough, however, that I wanted to ask her what was the matter right there in the bad hall light. I decided finally that while she had good reason to turn her nose up, she had no way of knowing it, so she was either supernaturally perceptive of character or flatly impolite, and I did not need worry about her. I hardly even knew about Tom and me well enough to be worried about me and his wife.

The bathroom was a Southern Living model with terry-cloth bibs and caps on the commode and an army of toiletries neatly marshaled into plastic trays and racks. I spotted a pink box of bubble bath and had a kooky urge to take one, but did not—I did not want to be to my neck in suds if Elaine attacked.

.  .  .

In the morning I had a conversation on the lawn with the girls as they waited to be taken somewhere. As if in response to their no-nitrate upbringing, they had begun, it looked, to get prematurely surly. They were little adults. I thought to try new utterance on them.

"Monsters, girls."

"Monsters what?"

"I think they're the thing."

They gave each other looks which contained concealed exasperation, quick passing glances designed to betray nothing. These were remarkable six-year-old women.

"I *am* a monster," one of them said. The other looked off, as if commenting without speaking, silently approving the sentiment. She would have pulled on a cigarette were they older and not no-nitrate. *She is*, her idle look said. *We are.* I wondered what they meant: could they possibly mean they *knew* they were premature not-children and thus monstrous?

"What do you mean?"

At this moment Elaine bounded out of the house with a picnic basket, binoculars, a bird book, and headed for the family car.

"You'd better *skip* over there and help her," the other girl said to the monster, and the monster did just that, brightly.

They were taking the girls to an "interpretive center" at a wildlife refuge and I declined Elaine's stiff invitation to go along. I declined Tom's somewhat sheepish invitation to ride with them to the bus station. Tom looked like he'd been thrashed.

"This *is* the bus station, Tom," I said, exacting from him no goofy mirth. He stood there near the car of loading women. I shook his hand and they left.

I walked through the polite suburb and found a larger street and then a larger street and the true bus station, and worked on placing Tom and the monsters into the fool/true-fool gradient all the way to Lafayette. As I have it, Tom is perhaps the worst victim to date, intelligent enough, unlike the Orphan, to have accepted someone else's notions of living correctly and to have applied considerable industry toward that end before sensing it was all downhill and all advised by amateurs. The girls were smart: bucking at an early age, wanting potato chips badly. They were duplicitous. "You'd better *skip* over there." They could run the fish camp, they could soothe the Veteran, they could act in any of Mary's plays. I could have kissed those little monsters, and I was certain that with due cover they'd have let me. One would have kissed while the other stood by smoking her imaginary cigarette, with a kind of jaw-out, hip-slung petulance, trying to locate something she knew they were not to find. They were as mad for Saturday cartoons and dangerous toys as was the Veteran for his phantom, and they were just beginning to show signs of denial.

A true scientist could run a control, a failed one

makes these speculations and, where no experiments can be had, makes these statements stridently, I suppose. So, mark my words: the little girls are tiny, early Veterans. They are being ruined by unwanted, forced purpose that seeks to free them of lateral waste. They are, as they say, monsters.

❦ / **E**very time I go home, I think suddenly how much more *sense* I had as a child, and that the years growing up in the house I am about to enter robbed me of that wit, as evidenced by my voluntary arrival of the moment. My father and I have developed a greeting which seems to acknowledge this solemn loss: whether I'm back from a month or a year away, he stands, extends his hand not very far toward me, broadly opened to receive the handshake, rather like a catcher's mitt held close to the body; and as we shake, meeting with elbows bent in order to retain leverage should we decide to Indian-wrestle, and gripping each other harder than desperate salesmen who squeeze rubber balls in their sleep, he will say, "Hey, bud." That seems to sum it all up neatly. You've lost *your* marbles, he says; I know, I gave the feeble things to you.

And you've lost *your* marbles, I squeeze back to him; I know, look how few you gave me.

We grin, not at each other but at the floor, departing from salesman's form.

While the notion of marbles is afoot, I look around for my mother. "She's not down yet," my father says.

He hands me a beer and we sit.

"What's going on?"

"Nothing."

This is code: Are you still wasting your life? Yes.

The silent ghost that is my mother appears at the foot of the stairs, extending around the doorjamb a preposterously tall, narrow glass that suggests a flared vase. My father looks at the glass and waits, as I'm sure he would not do in my absence, for her to explain herself. Even though the glass is empty, she has trouble balancing it, because she holds it at the narrow base, the only place her tiny, bony hand can grip it. It leads her, like an animal going for drink, into the kitchen.

"More juice?" she says.

"I think you've had enough."

"He's so *handsome*," she says, about me, whom she has recognized only partly: I am her handsome son, she knows, but I am not yet her son come to visit.

"I thought, just another," she says. "Since . . ."

Here she has begun to recognize my visit: *since* my handsome son has come to see me. She now sits and pats the chair next to her, where I go and sit. She holds my face as I take her glass. "He's so handsome." We kiss, which is perhaps the most difficult aspect of a home visit, because since her trouble began she has applied lipstick around, not on, her lips, in a wide ovoid tour of her face suggestive all at once of Emmett Kelly and blackface minstrels and topographical contour maps. She has gone in for odd shades of orange lipstick since this novel application began; it gives her the look of an aging peach.

"Maybe some of the high stuff, too," she says to my father, who is filling her vase with orange juice. He hesitates. He looks at me, as if to say he is a better keeper than giving her another drink would suggest, and I give him a little *why not* shrug, to suggest I know he's a better keeper, and so we agree on her drinking and he adds some vodka. Frankly I have never seen why she shouldn't have all she wants; it only changes her physical dexterity, and that not much. I do not even know the official diagnosis, though I know there is one. My father maintains simply that she is "sick." "Premature senility" seemed to suffice in the beginning, but today I am sure there are more specific names, if not more specific treatment.

She sits back with her foot-high drink, the only glass she will have, and my father and I let her concentrate on it before we start our tape.

"How's school?"

"Fine. I'm not *in* it, though, exactly."

"What do you mean?"

"I got fed up."

He hands me another beer. I hand it back. "I'm in training."

"For what?"

"Life."

"Good luck."

Now that I have indicated I may *not* become a professor, the only natural end, in his mind, of a higher degree, he is ready to allow some merit accrue to the profession which was altogether lacking while he thought me pursuing it.

"In the Depression, professors were the only guys with work. They had *good* jobs."

"I'm sure." We are close to the end and best part of the tape, and I can't stand it, so I jump his lines. "Life is fifty-one percent, like you say."

"You're damned *straight*." His emphasis delivers the meaning: again, he means I am *not* straight.

Generally these conversations—or this conversation, it does not vary—amount to a slow but surefooted indictment of whatever I am doing, and they are a bit irritating because before now I have always been more or less applying myself in ways more or less indicated, I felt, by a natural pursuit of self-aggrandizing going up in the world. But tonight, for the first time, his accusations are correct, though he doesn't know it, and because they are correct, our little play is not irritating.

"What I've been doing," I say, "—and I will have that beer—is women in squalid quarters who are all about Mom's age. Been fun." My father apparently senses an extraordinary turn, which a taunt like my revelation finally is, and surprises my mother with yet another towering drink, which she bites down on like a snake volunteering venom into a toxin funnel.

"Mmm," she says. "High stuff, too."

He shakes his head with a small laugh, and he realizes we are not going to fight because I'm not going to defend, I'm going to attack.

"Fifty-one percent, I think, is better at about nineteen. I'm playing nineteen. I have a friend up the road chasing armadillos with a Geiger counter. He's hitting ninety-five percent."

My father compresses his lips, pushes them out a bit. This speech is about his credo—the speculator's/hustler's credo—of life and business. If you win fifty-one percent, you're in the black. The presence of the credo is the subterranean suggestion, ever present, that I take over the oil-pipe business.

"He's so *hand*some." We look at her, at each other.

"You're right," he says—to me, about Tom's ninety-five percent, not my looks. He is not sincere.

While my mother balances her drink—how she came to be served exclusively in this ridiculous and difficult container I do not know—my father and I make a drink for ourselves. The strong whiskey makes me dizzy, as if a wave of water has gone through the room. I am prepared, as at no time before, to deny completely all injunction, pressure to assume the family business, which topic is just beneath the surface of all our percent patter.

Before, my refusal has been vague, I have managed simply to delay the event. Tonight I am possessed of this confident, sliding-away strength, and I am not going to delay, to put it off, I'm going to deny the inheritance because . . . because *I no longer trust women my age*. That is the thought that comes to me as we watch my mother totter her vase of high stuff to her orange face. Pine-Sol and Havana Carlisle's legendary cigars (my father has lit a cigarillo) come to me. The entire life reaction series of human bondings and splittings has had something to do with my not taking the family business. It is the artificial center someone would have me assume.

At that moment I thought of Mary and Wallace, and of my own mother and how she had changed from someone not like them to someone very much like them. I've liked my mother a whole lot more since she became daft, for where she is dotty and funny now, she was presumptuous and full of conviction before, and if one's preferring a crippled mental state to the normal precedent, particularly his own mother's, is perverse, then so be it. It is just another index of the magnitude of the effects of the series.

I get ready to tell my father, "I refuse the business because I refuse these young twit broads full of purpose"—something actually that rational is on my tongue—when my mother says, out of the blue, to him, "You'd better get ready."

It startles me. Can she know? Can she perceive mental states now that hers is largely gone?

"The beauty parlor isn't open until 9:30," my father says.

"Then we'd better be ready."

My mother has an appointment at her beauty parlor every day of the week. They oblige her there, with, among other services, the application of her lipstick as she likes it, and when she emerges looking like Emmett Kelly with a blue Virginia Graham hairdo, they assure her how good she looks in condescending tones.

"We'll be ready," I say.

"Do you," she says, turning to me, "have a license to meddle?"

This is a bit of the old girl. These vodkas are having a restorative effect.

"Yes," I say.

"It's *expired*," she says. To my father: "Your *son's* got a meddling license." She means, I think, to emphasize the *your*, to saddle him with me, but in missing the emphasis she indicts my sex, she invokes the daughter she never was able to have, and so you cannot know finally if the emphasis is misplaced or simply badly timed. She does this curious emphasis often.

My father and I keep quiet waiting for her little tempest to pass, probably both now doubting the wisdom of allowing her the three towering cocktails.

"I know what lips are," she says, grinning, as if to acknowledge she has been naughty in this passing assault, "but what's *stick*?" Thus she is restored, occupied by lipstick, one of her two or three central preoccupations (the beauty parlor, the high stuff) since her illness set in. In a moment she'll be again deciding I'm handsome beyond all rational measure. By her flare-up, my father is spared my kook speech.

When they retire I wander about the house: it is a blend of low ranch and tall Georgian, which means twenty small columns across the broad, split-level front, where once four tall columns would have been. The rooms are museum set pieces, matched collections of antiques assembled by my mother.

In the kitchen I am surprised to find my father back down, having another drink, his face a brick-red hue and his lips aligned in a tall, narrow pursing, as if carefully stacked up for the sake of neatness. I get a beer.

Without turning his head to look at me, he says, "You're not doing *anything*." Now the lips are pressed out into a grim line, a shade lighter than when they'd been in the warehouse position.

"No, sir. For once you are correct."

He makes no move.

"In fact," I say, "I'm doing *less* than anything." I

have noticed that in my dealings with him I am invariably cast back into an adolescent kind of smartness, and he responds in kind by pretending to hear me out without listening, waiting to tell me where I went wrong.

"You don't need any more beer." In our family, one is never accused of drinking to excess until the accuser is on the floor himself, from where he will utter his sudden call for temperance.

"I'm going to wait up and talk to the yardmen."

He looks at me with true alarm.

"What?"

"Fuck with them."

"Those are good, steady boys."

I go out into my old room, a garage apartment designed to look from the outside like an old, detached Southern kitchen. It is set up for poker now—a beautiful felt table and chips on a lazy Susan and a fully stocked bar. I get a small cooler and pack it with beer and get a canvas deck chair and plan to set up camp for the night on the tennis court. *You're not doing anything.* I thought, by God, to prove it.

I walk the tennis court, cracking acorns on the deep green composition surface made nearly black by the shadows of the oaks. In the early morning, hours before my father takes my mother to the beauty parlor, but only a bit sooner than she begins to pester him to do so, two black men about fifty years old, whom my father without malice calls The Boys, will arrive to rake the yard. I wish The Boys would sweep the courts as well, sweep these acorns going off like firecrackers out here at three in the morning. I pop, I skid, I skate. I lose track of time, I think—perhaps out of drinking shape without Mary—because it is suddenly dawning and I see The Boys arrive and set up to rake, nearly invisible in their green uniforms in the fog, talking as low and gently as if they were fishing.

As a child I thought The Boys were a constant two men and only now realize that they change over rapidly, supplied by a lawn service with access to an apparently inexhaustible supply of quiet, early-rising blacks. To my father I believe they *are* a constant team—The Boys.

Suddenly my exact position—as reagent, binding surfactant—in the reaction series of life gets clearer. Since Wallace had echoed Mary, certainly since Tom "accidentally" appeared on my personal bus driver's route in a town of his fond bestial memories, I could tell that the series was self-governing and rapidly moving to inexorable conclusions. But now I thought to look at the business bond by bond—to pull the test tube off my head and see things molecularly, as it were. I watched The Boys. Before my very unscientific eyes they were aligned with all the better fools—James and Ebert, of course, but if they did not suggest Wallace and Napoleon out there in a fog of low wages, I'd be damned, and I thought of Hazel and Bruce, and they, The Boys, were quite likely accomplished actors: they were not distracted by the self-centeredness of the Orphan and the other true fools. These are the thoughts you can have, drunk at five in the morning, skating on acorns on your private tennis court.

But I saw that it was data, and it felt like nearly final data. I have seen the better scientists I know— Friedeman can do it—sense magically when enough experimentation has been done, when data are yet an uncollated mess and no rational measure could suggest quitting time. I had that feeling watching The Boys rake in the fog.

I exploded acorns on the way toward them, and one of them saw me and stopped, looking at me as if I were a deer or something not seen in the last twenty years. I held my beer up to him in greeting.

"You guys want a cold one?"

"Naw."

"It's all right."

"Know."

"Yes, it is."

"Say *know.*"

"Really, man. I'm the—"

"Say I *know* iss all right. Old man himself making us the offer. Talk trash."

"He was?"

He raked a small pile of leaves up.

"In that case, I withdraw the offer."

"Better."

My silly little mood was ruined, but it was good

to know you can't rout fifty-year-old men just because other fifty-year-old men call them The Boys. I shook the yardman's hand. He gave me the standard black limp, so limp you don't see how it could be remotely attached to the muscular arm that extends it. I waved over my head to them as I left the yard. They were indifferent.

A little sanity at six in the morning demonstrated by men raking leaves for life—by men in full possession of nothing—jotted down fine in the blurry data column I was filling.

At ten we sat in the formal dining room at my mother's request and had what she calls brunch. It is no different from breakfast, and the dining room is not used even for holidays now, but for my visits it is brunch in the dining room. Beyond these alterations of decorum, she ignores me.

She is got up—suit, pearl choker, matching shoes and bag—to go to the beauty parlor. Between courses, served from the kitchen by the maid, she asks my father the time.

"Don't ask me again," he finally says. He says this without anger, but it sets her off on a vengeful course anyway.

She looks at me and catches me examining the design in the china. "That *china's* expensive," she says, looking then directly at my father.

It is a reasonable cue for one to guard himself, set

himself for a blow of the absurd. Her emphasis on *china* rather than *expensive* is a signal that what follows won't be easy to track. But my father does not prepare for the blow, nor will he share a flicker of condescension with me.

"This plate," my mother says, slyly touching my father's plate, "cost four hundred dollars." She quickly jerks her finger back, as if the plate has suddenly gotten hot.

She looks at her finger. Or pretends to. I notice that she actually looks at me while holding her finger in front of her face. She wants a sign, one hair of a reaction, to launch into finer, higher absurdity—to "have a fit," in my father's parlance. This is, I find, remarkable—she is perfectly and vigorously logical in the way she can scale into a *tour de force* of mindlessness. While the content of her fit will be nuts, the form will be logical, and it has made me wonder—my father apparently does not—if her sickness is not partly or part-time voluntary.

She still looks at her finger. "We *had* the four hundred and we had to *buy* the plate." This is a complex accusation. I've heard, as I say, its form before, and she means, I think, that even though we had the money, we were not old-family and therefore did not already own the china and *had* to buy it—with new money, thereby invalidating in certain senses our right to even have the heirloom china.

She is saying, I think, that she was a country-club,

new-millionaire's wife who wasted herself in pursuit of a status that specifically could not be bought. If I throw her into the fool/true-fool gradient, she appears to be not unlike the Veteran—someone gave her a false center to pursue and she did and discovered finally it was hollow. She had a houseful of River Road furniture and no family name to match it. She has a houseful of dead fucking niggers. She was self-important until one day she discovered she was not important. This, I think, at table, at brunch—and who knows but that she is mocking even now—is what has unleveled her.

On the sideboard I notice a postcard—out of place in the unused room—and lean to look at it; as I do, my mother says, "It's for you."

"It's what?"

"Read it. Ladyfriend—but *I* don't have a license to meddle."

The card is a photo of a romantic scene very much like the one of Mary in the Sunday supplement, and I see before anything else *M.C.B.* signed on the back.

*Muhv—*
*Garden restored. Miss you more than like. Got*
*sillymental in Fla. (about Stump—don't tell Hoop)*
*and messed up. Give call. Tunkie Friedeman gave*
*address. Says he knows you'll be back in the sun soon,*
*ha ha. Said to tell you that. ? Drop by? Love—*

# A Woman
## Named Drown

Friedeman? What in the world was going on? *Tunkie* Friedeman? *Conspiracy theory* entered my mind. This was no damned Brownian powder-blown drift. I felt like Mia Farrow in *Rosemary's Baby*.

Then again, was it only that Mary and Friedeman knew each other and somehow discovered—did I tell Mary I worked for a Friedeman and she held her no-bio tongue? Yes. I told her I worked for a nut. She smiled. She knew him. But how did she know I'd come home? She didn't. Chanced it. A small endothermic bonding 238 bondings down the thousandfold series that was evolving me unto some end.

I recalled an early chemistry professor I had who seemed to have relied entirely upon his sense of smell in achieving his considerable academic station. On emeritus status, he was employed to interest freshmen in the magic of chemistry—almost the alchemy of chemistry—its colors, its aromatic delights, even its poetry. His chemistry was numberless, headache-free, earthy, approximate, elegant—a chemistry that seduced worried freshmen. You may call dicopper oxide, he'd say, cuprous oxide, and copper oxide, cu*pric*. You may, as the English do, refer to al-you-*min*ium. Bleach is sodium hypohalite. He'd waft a tube to his Old World nose, hold it to the light—*glacial* acetic acid (you may call it condensed vinegar), or another tube, product of a spuming reaction—sniff—why, it's old *methyl ethyl ketone*. What's that brown stuff in there? Some suspicious student would ask. That, the emeritus Nose Chemist would say, that is nothing, some trash.

I felt then, with the postcard, as if that was the only kind of chemist I could reasonably be in this life chemistry—it would have to be by instinct and it would have to be relied on well. Mary's card impressed me as not unlike unidentified brown precipitate in a reaction too complex to probe further in the particular. It was not *trash*, but it was finally distracting to know more about it. Mary and Tunkie Friedeman. Were they lovers? How far back could reactions in the life series be said to go?

"What time is it? I'd better get ready. Are you ready?"

"Dad, are you still selling the company?" He looks at me, happy not to have to answer her. "You still planning to sell?"

"I have buyers," he says.

"Who's running it?"

"It's on auto-pilot." He doesn't want to talk about it.

"Would it still be good not to sell?"

"Smart not to."

"Isn't my appointment at eleven?" my mother says.

"Mother," he says, "the appointment is at *noon*. It's *always* at noon."

"*Are you ready?*"

He turns from her, stone-faced. Something happens

to me. Before I can say it, my mother announces, "I have osteopsoriasis."

"Don't sell," I say.

"What?"

"Osteopsoriasis. It's new."

"I'll do it," I say. "Give me a year."

"A year? Are you serious?"

"He's so *hands*ome."

Very gravely, as if we have just signed a world armistice, he stands and rounds the corner of the table, his hand extended in an arc much wider than the catcher's-mitt position ceremoniously toward me. We shake.

"Mother," he orders, "*get in the car.* You don't want to be late."

"Not *today*," she says. She fairly jogs out of the house.

"I'll have to drive her around for an hour." He grins, the first I've seen. "Do we understand each other?" he says.

"I think we do," I say, not knowing yet why I've said what I've said.

"Why are you in those clothes?"

I persuade him to drop me off at the bus station— he suggests I take a plane—and we part on very good terms under the G O B I G R E D marquee, his engine running and my mother primping in the rearview, smiling at herself.

❦  /  On the way to Knoxville I considered the proper use of new utterance, its true relation, if any, to the formulations I have been borne along on. It seems now that new utterance is perhaps the linguistic equivalent of the kind of living that takes into account backward as well as forward motion. The maker of new utterance is taking a chance that he will not close the gap toward meaning, that he may in fact widen it, as the foolish living I've come to appreciate chances the same failure to advance and may indeed set one back. On the final bus home I regarded myself as a kind of Havana Carlisle willing to tell things anew—willing to wave my cigar about and be misinterpreted, if that was the cost.

I immediately went to Friedeman's office and with no delay found him.

"Tunkie," I said.

He looked up from his desk, his face a wave of recognition and, I thought, put-on happy-to-see-you mirth. He solemnly stood and came around to me, extending both hands. He said, "My son, the fire is renewed?" His manner was altogether suggestive of a *Benedict* rather than a *Tunkie*.

"I have a year in which to be consumed by it, Father."

He then looked at me with what I took to be real delight, and I think it was delight in my assuming a penitant's role, which made to me altogether more sense about him. His Baptism *was* a polite mockery, a new utterance *he* played with.

"What in hell are you doing in my brother's clothes?"

For a moment I was confused, thinking he was yet in the charade and referring to some ecclesiastical brother. Then: he did not mean, did he, Stump?

"I'd know those clothes anywhere."

I sat down and we had a talk, the result of which was my concluding that there is room in this world for either a whole lot of coincidence or a *whole* lot of design, call it what you will. The short of it was that Tunkie and Stuart (Stump) Friedeman were wild men and Connie Baker a wild woman (they all called her Connie, as had Hoop; only I, her no-bio boy, had used the formal Mary) and they were in love and Stump "won." At least he had for a time.

Now, it would seem, Tunkie was the one to claim spoils, though I did not learn, or care to know, any of it. I was still, it seemed in his office, as now, on no-bio status, and I thought it certainly best he remain specifically so with respect to Mary and me.

"I have a year."

We discussed my research—his research—and I was surprisingly clear about where I'd left off, and we concurred that we should be able to determine the particular boron-lithium mechanic we sought well within a year and that I would go free with a signed degree.

"Tunkie," I said at the end, still incredulous that a Dr. Friedeman could become a fast-car teenager named Tunkie before my very eyes.

"Time is a marvel," he said, standing, concluding our intimacies. "I know full well you are *enough* of a scientist." We were back to science. It was nice to have struck a gentleman's agreement as we had in a world of spin accelerators and Fourier analyzers and computers called NERDS.

So that is how I came finally to take notes again, and again notes of science in a blue-gridded engineering notebook, on a heavy slate lab bench, down which I sight a tiny army of test tubes in white polypropylene racks taking aliquots from an automatic pipette. It is a tiny induction into service: the stiff fellows at glassy attention taking their inoculations like the best of soldiers. I will march them into chromatographs, fire electrons at them, freeze them. Some will step back and some will step forward. Together we will answer a question about a structure so small the ink of this *word* could insulate it against the light of day for a thousand years.

Titration (that is what the aliquots are about) is precisely the model for my conclusions about loss and gain. This came to me immediately after I talked to Friedeman and that afternoon set up a run. It is precisely a series of excesses and shortages that determines the resting point—I have been on a tour of titration, admiring the true titrators of life as I found them.

I was in this rumination, deciding it was a bit forced to carry further, that it was better to conclude my investigations somewhat less specifically, after the fashion of, say, the Nose Chemist, when an extraordinary thing happened. Minnie, the building's maid, came in and counted out change and asked if I'd go get her a bottle of wine.

"Ain't *seen* you in a time," she said. "You been sick?"

"No, Minnie. Took a trip."

"That's nice."

I took her change and left for the wine. This was not unusual. Minnie—a black woman, but so light-skinned students debate her race—is a long story herself. Among the pleasures she affords folk, besides her

speaking nicely and well to you as she sweeps under
your very stool late at night, is that of stopping the
nonsense you are about and sending you to the campus
bar ostensibly to get her some wine. I am probably one
of four or five trusted wine couriers. After her order,
at this time of evening—after talking to Friedeman and
setting up, it was late—I could expect to meet her on
the roof for a drink.

What is extraordinary is what happened in the
bar. I saw a fellow student, alone, and joined him with
my beer and Minnie's bottle. He and I were peripherally
acquainted, I did not know him well. He was known
chiefly for his hair, which is red and wild, visible at a
half mile—a hirsute monument to 1969. He is also
known for his participation in a scandalous *ménage à
trois* involving two other graduate students, and for his
generally pleasant demeanor (he is sometimes referred
to as the Pacifist). I sat down.

We simply drank—Men at Science—after the
initial greeting. He was watery in the eye; I concluded
his pitcher of beer might not have been the first. As I
finished my own mug, he refilled it, generously washing the table with suds. The spill floated a folded card
on the table advertising a new product called Wine
without Alcohol.

"Wine without alcohol!" the Pacifist shouted.
"That's like—like women without *sex!*"

Suddenly I knew him from somewhere, knew more

about him than I thought. He was a Veteran! He was a drunk, academic, foot-stomping Veteran. As one would with the Veteran himself, I held my cards.

I recalled once standing with him on a fourth-floor balcony watching students come and go, and we happened to witness his girl leaving campus with the other corner of the notorious triad. My man appeared to be the afternoon man. The other fellow, who resembles less a hippie than a young athletic coach, had her, as the mill had it, for the night. We stood on the balcony and watched Coach and the shared lover leave campus.

"Looks rough," I said.

"You can say *that* again," he said. He said it with such fidelity to its customary comic use that I nearly laughed. He was not about to laugh, though.

Now, in the bar, I was sure his condition was owing to the Coach and the Devoted being home together. I did not dare broach it. In the noise of darts and jukebox and pizza orders he started telling me about doing acid.

"I was in Matagorda, Texas, man. I dropped some acid and got in my tent and ate an apple. These *crabs* came up to the tent. I started feeding them pieces of apple. They *ate* the *apple*, man. They were huge. Claws like Japanese *monster movies*. It was wild."

"I bet."

"They'd run up, you know, grab the apple, and *run away!*" He laughed. Despite his momentary laugh, I still thought he looked as wrung out as the Veteran.

*"Wine without alcohol!"* he yelled again, noticing the card as if for the first time.

"No human sorrow," he suddenly intoned, *"ever stopped the world."*

I looked at him. I was right, then, apparently, about his preoccupation, but I still did not know what to say. He poured me another beer.

"Thanks."

"You need it."

"I need it?"

"Man, it's okay. The word's out about—" He stopped. He meant Dr. Eminence in Norway.

"That?" I said. It—she—truly felt a million years ago and a million miles away. "Shit." I dismissed it all with a gesture which he smiled at, as if he thought me bluffing. I realized we had a bit more in common than I'd thought. We'd both hung up on bright schoolgirls, at the least. And to, it looked, no profit. The next thing is what stunned me.

"You going to drink that?" he said, referring to Minnie's bottle.

"It's for Minnie."

*"Hey!* Minnie is a *quality person!"*

I could not respond. It was not simply that I had not impugned her in any way to provoke his defense, and it was not that I could not have agreed more with him and so felt doubly strange being accused of impugning her. It was that he was regarding Minnie, in his present lovelorn straits, exactly as I had come to regard Mary and Hazel and Wallace, and even my own mother, and Minnie indeed was one of them, and, indeed—it was too much—he was, it looked, on the brink of a plunge identical to my own. *The events were duplicable.* I could prove my results. The interlude had necessity, was not random, was not lunatic.

"She's a *what*?" I said.

"She's a *quality person!*" he shouted again, and I thought he was going to come over the table.

I shouted at him, "You can say *that* again!" and started laughing, and he, after a minute, did, too.

I left him there, no doubt in my mind that he was launched in his own series of titrations against and away from a certain sort of preoccupation.

Minnie and her custodial partner, Earl, were on the roof when I got there. We sat on the parapet, where we could see Earl's car parked in the vapor lighting of the loading dock. Earl was most careful of his car, which he had painted aerosol-can gold. It had the look, from where we were above it, of a huge, dull moth on the ground.

"It's all right, honey," Minnie was saying to Earl, when nothing at all suggested that Earl was concerned. She held my arm then, as if to say further assistance would not be necessary. Earl looked at his car, wet-eyed, mumbling in his high, singing tones nothing anyone but Minnie can understand. He talks like a man with his tongue cut out, and yet every gesture—the whole demeanor—looks rational. No one has a clue as to what's wrong with him, what happened.

Minnie and I got into one of our discussions of bigotry, a frequent topic.

"Mr. Harry Truman, I believe," she said, "was a *spigot*, but at least a straight-up one. I say spigot because this is no world for name-calling."

She extended her glass for wine. In the vapor light our teeth were already purple.

I put the wine into a mound of gravel, attempting to insulate it: cooling wet green glass in gravel.

"Entropy, Minnie. The wine has a bad case of entropy." She will like new utterance, I thought.

"I *love* entropy."

Earl was studying his furry car, a worried tune coming from him.

I said to Minnie: "Minnie."

"*Yeah*yess," she said.

"Have you always swept floors?"

"No, sir. I have not always swept floors." She said this with a wistful ease that reminded me of Havana Carlisle—as if she were content with a cigar and a sunny street and a secret. "That," she said, "is my *prerogative*."

"I know it is," I said.

She sat on the parapet, not inelegantly, with her legs crossed. The Carlisle connection was not idle— why did the reaction series put before me these landmark blacks, and why now what I took to be half-a-black? She was not unlike my mother in the scheme: she was perhaps an isomer, an identical compound in a different structure, to my mother. I thought this quite literally, trusting that it was not strictly a matter of the wine and my purple teeth.

She was isomer to my mother: half black and totally prescient, and my mother, who'd been told she was, in the River Road scheme of things, equivalently only half white, was totally distracted. Earl came over to Minnie and faced her, moving to his own noise in a little rumba motion. I noticed the wine was low, and in the same instant I saw the Pacifist emerge from the shadows on the ground.

"Get one of these," I called to him. He looked up.
"What?"

"With alcohol." I pointed to the bottle, which I held up. He saw Minnie. He turned abruptly back into the shadows. Impressed with the telegraphy of drunks, I turned to discover Minnie and Earl dancing.

Beyond the notion of people with purple teeth dancing a cappella on a roof, the thing to see was Earl. What wasn't coming out of his mouth so clearly was with complete brilliance and precision coming out of his feet. He was leading Minnie very strongly in a fast honky-tonk kind of swing, Minnie bandying about on the spins like Lucille Ball, Earl like a matador, not disturbing a speck of pea gravel. Minnie's legs flew up for balance, her head back; Earl engineered the next turn,

Teflon man. I had never seen a better dancer than Earl.

It was a magical scene. They slowed down a bit. Minnie recovered some form and suggested not so much a slapstick Lucy as a proud, regal Lena Horne. Earl mumbled something very high to her and she said, "You're welcome. Thank *you*, Earl," and they parted.

The Pacifist was on the roof. "What are y'all *doing* up here?"

"Hey, sugar," Minnie said, sitting back on the parapet.

"Hello, Minnie," the Pacifist said, rather formally, I thought, perhaps still defending her honor from before.

Minnie extended her glass toward the new bottle, which the Pacifist and I went for.

"Man, all the way down there you can tell you guys are titrating with the purple indicator," the Pacifist said. It was parlance in the department to speak of drinking as titrating, and this Rit-dye wine—the only kind we could get on campus—as "the purple indicator."

"I thought that was *tit rate*," Minnie said. "You boys is always *tit rating* everything." I looked at her: it was hard to tell if she was joking.

The Pacifist didn't care. "We *are!*" he shouted, as overly loud as he'd been in the bar. "My girlfriends never have *any* tits."

"That's all right, mine don't, either," Minnie said.

This put the Pacifist into a knee slap. He came out of it teary-eyed. "That's a good one, Minnie."

"I'll tell you a good one," Minnie said. The Pacifist slid down inside the parapet wall next to her in the attitude of a child at storytime. He was a truly unhappy dude.

"Mandy Smith was with the ladies down at the Baptist Ladies' Aid, you know," Minnie said. "And she says, Girls, don't tell Opal Brown about the bazaar because Opal Brown don't have no class. She doesn't know Opal Brown walk up behind her.

"Opal Brown says, Say what? Opal Brown don't have no class? Who bought the genuine simulated crushed-velvet carpet for the pastor to walk on? Opal Brown, that's who. Who bought the dime-store expensive red glasses for the communion? Opal Brown, that's who. *No class? Sheeeit.*"

The Pacifist started laughing hysterically, sliding over onto the gravel, holding his sides. Before my very eyes I thought I saw the initial reaction in the commencement of his tour that would be identical to mine: when he could, he looked at Minnie with what I took to be sober awe. He was stunned, if I've got the entire thing right, to notice the pleasure afforded him by this most noncustodial of janitors (the second one in these series—James in mine, Minnie in his). She had startled him as I'd been startled by Mary and no-bio gins and flowers and billiards.

Why did these wanderings—they were *not* Brownian meanders, I was convinced, looking at our purple-
mouthed gang—seem to make use of older women
early on, and why—I thought of Ebert-James-The
Boys—blacks? And why, now, in Minnie, what appeared to be a person of both camps offering a powerful hybrid vigor? Perhaps it was having set up a
hundred stiff titrations hours before and drawn a table
to accommodate results, but I began to speculate then
and there in a fashion altogether too rigorous for the
Nose Chemist to approve.

What my reaction series had come to, or brought
me to, or made of me, I'm sure is better known at some
considerable analytical remove from the way I will
have to know my pipette doughboys. I am, perhaps,
for example, just some odd precipitate that fell out of
a larger event, not the principal product, not practically
identifiable, not important. I knew, however, on the
roof, that I had had drinks with Minnie before my trip,
and the drinks now were entirely another affair. Before,
I might have humored her—without condescension and
with considerable honest pleasure taken in her company, but it was a humoring all the same. Now I was
prepared to have her humor me: *I* was the one on the
roof with the improbably high propensity to dalliance,
the incalculable willingness to step sideways and backward before forward.

I decided to call it the anti-actualization quotient.
Looking at Earl and Minnie and the Pacifist and a

campus full of shadows, the function defined itself as ambition, times self-centered custodial purpose, divided by one's natural opportunities for going up in the world.

People started to key out nicely. The Orphan, I decided, was the Low Quotient Standard and Ebert was the opposite Definitive Standard: his natural opportunities for going up so low that no matter what his ambition, his sense of self-preservation, his anti-actualization value would remain astronomically high.

James is a peg lower (lower value equals higher *actualization* potential), having developed sufficient verbal skills to go up to a secure, ironic position of the deliberately idle, grandly titled factotum. Blacks in general, I thought, despite legislation and whatnot, sense such low values in their denominators, their true opportunities for worldly advance, that they automatically adjust to a reasonably low sense of self-importance to keep things, as it were, in balance (like their blood pressure); and their ambition, which can be high, becomes moot. (Sweeping floors, Minnie says, is her "prerogative.")

An opposite kind of case, with a nearly equal final quotient, is a Bobby Cherry: these good-old-boy gas-station dandies have high opportunities, and though their honest ambition is middling, their sense of self-importance is so *extremely high* that the entire quotient climbs into range with the blacks. It is these identical anti-actualization quotients that keep the tush-hogs hating the humbler blacks.

And so one can go on. I wanted to rush from the roof and get some graph paper and begin keying people out, but Minnie and the Pacifist, talking as if at the late stages of a loud party, brought me to. The Pacifist was no longer morose. He was en route, in his series. Before Minnie said *No class*, he was as hooked on the parade of pert tits and young brains as I was—these onward debutantes of science are the arbiters of low anti-actualization. His Shared Devoted and my Dr. Eminence give us headaches and heartaches trying to keep up. High ambitions, bloated importance, normal *natural* opportunity (higher if you figure affirmative action)— they balance into an egregious, self-aggrandizing machine that eats people up. These modern whippets are climbing the ladder of success busting the rungs out. They hurl us who would pursue them into courting widows while wearing the deceased's pastels and falling in love with the maid.

Minnie smoking on the parapet, the Pacifist sitting on the roof with his head not a foot from her lap, Earl becalmed into a swaying surveillance of his car, I shaped the gravel around the wine. We looked like a guerrilla camp.

And so what is it, the older-women thing, that put the Pacifist and me into our revolts? Discovery of discoveries, looking at Minnie as I am, it comes to me: they have adjusted anti-actualization quotients like the blacks have. Thus, Minnie doubly is the queen bee that she is in this universe of practiced loss.

Mary was like a ball glove handed to you in the seventh inning, used by someone else during the critical innings, and you get to play when the game is nearly won or lost with a trained glove that promises to be error-free. She was frayed, she was wrinkled, she had a cotton-candy softness, but all in all, she was a package of reticence and careless ease so correctly balanced I had never been so attracted to a person in my life.

"*Sheeeeeit*," the Pacifist suddenly said, going into a fit again. Minnie grabbed his hair and shook it gently and let go; the Pacifist looked up, around, to see what the pressure had been. I was pouring her another wine and he did not know she had touched him.

Things were, at this moment, clear and not clear to me. Overall, I had taken a little downside sabbatical that had shown me something I would find it best to know only as the Nose Chemist knew his ketones: with Havana Carlisle in the back of my mind, I could inherit a two million net deal with enough grace that I would not worry about acquiring a $400 River Road plate, not haze a yardman—not much more, finally, was certain. Havana kept appearing to me: instead of cigar-waving down the main street of his town in Missouri, he was waving his cigar across my crushed-shell trucking lot. He was telling the company: Let's raise our anti-actualization quotients to comfortable levels and go on about our business with these pipes.

The world seemed a place of improbable wild hope. I told my father I will run his business—my business—and all I see, all I can hold probable about that, is gathering these fools together and seeing how far we can go on two million dollars. Bonaparte washes trucks, whistling shrilly all the live-long day, and *drives*. Wallace dispatches trucks by heaving darts into the territory board. The Veteran watches the grounds at night. My bus driver takes a load of oil pipe, and another, here, and there, and never has to return. When I get ambitious, I'll have Tunkie Friedeman come down and formulate a revolutionary synthetic that will set the pace for the next generation of pipe.

And Mary. I resolve, in the morning, to drop by. One does not, when calling on Mary, need pause to buy flowers.